FAMILY SECRETS

STACY CLAFLIN

FAMILY SECRETS
BRANNON HOUSE #2
by Stacy Claflin
http://www.stacyclaflin.com

Receive free books from the author sign up here: https://stacyclaflin.com/newsletter/

1

Kenzi

The wind whips my hair and fat rain droplets splash on my cheeks, nose, and forehead. I cover my face with my arm, trying to protect my makeup, and race toward the looming structure ahead. My foot lands in the middle of a puddle, and it sploshes up my leg, leaving a trail of dirt from my knee down to my purple stilettos.

I knew I should've worn black. That's what people wear to funerals, but my niece Ember and I decided to celebrate my sister's life instead of focusing on her untimely demise, so we asked everyone to wear the bright colors she loved—a decision I suddenly regret.

A deafening boom of thunder shakes through me, making my ears ring. Two streaks of lightning weave together behind the tall church building. This was not at all what we pictured for Claire's service. It's August—the hottest and driest month of the summer. But this is also a suburb of Seattle, which means it can rain at any time.

I force myself to run as fast as I can in these shoes before I end up completely soaked. At least we're early, so I'll have a little time to dry off and fix my hair and makeup. As I push open the heavy door, I take a deep breath.

Thunder claps behind me, and I yank the door closed. I resist the temptation to shake off like a dog. Instead, I pull away the long dark hair plastered to my face and shake my arms.

Ember comes into the foyer, and her eyes widen as she looks me over. "Is it raining?"

"No, I thought I'd take a second shower between here and the car."

She snickers. "But you found the bracelet? Grandma won't stop asking about it."

I nod, then pull it out of my purse and hand it to her. "It was under the passenger seat. Do you mind giving it to her while I fix my makeup?"

"Yeah, sure. Do you know if Jack is coming?"

"Jack?" Sounds vaguely familiar, but I draw a blank. "Is he one of the lawyers from your mom's firm?"

Ember shrugs. "Grandma keeps saying Jack should be here by now."

"Just humor her. We're lucky she halfway remembers us today."

"Halfway?" My niece lifts a brow. "She thinks I'm her sister."

"I know, but at least she can be here today. The way she was acting last week, I really didn't think this would be possible." She'd had a meltdown when we visited her at the home because her pudding was the wrong flavor. There would be no pudding after the service. I made sure of that.

"Just hurry." Ember turns toward the sanctuary. "Here's your bracelet, Grandma!"

I shiver as I make my way to the bathroom. The mirror proves I don't look as bad as I thought. My legs and shoes got the worst of it. I may have to pull my hair back instead of letting it fall freely down my back, but at least I won't have to redo my makeup.

After I remove the dirt from my legs and shoes, I check the time. Twenty minutes before guests will start to arrive, but there are always those who arrive early, so I need to make sure everything is ready now.

One more look in the mirror—I'm going to let my hair dry before I decide what to do with it—and I head back to the foyer. I check the table with memorabilia from Claire's life.

A wave of sadness washes over me. This is all that's left of my sister's life, all I'll ever really know. I never reached out to her, and now I'll never get to. I push aside the thoughts and focus on how I can make a difference in her daughter's life. Ember has already started to relax around me, a stranger until the day her mom was murdered, and I'm growing in my role as her guardian. It isn't the life either of us saw for ourselves, her without a mom and me at only twenty-five raising her, but we'll make it work. Not just because we have to, but because we're Brannon women. We've got this.

I straighten a framed photo on the table and flip through a scrapbook from Claire's childhood. No pictures of me. I didn't come along until she was fifteen. Ember's age now.

She appears from the doorway. "Save me!"

"Okay, okay. I got lost in thought."

Ember throws me an exasperated glance. "She's telling me about where Mom was conceived."

I burst out laughing.

"It's not funny!"

"And it's also probably not what really happened. She thinks the Vietnam war is still happening."

"Just hurry. People are going to mess all that stuff up, anyway. We already got pictures when it looked perfect."

We make our way down the aisle, and I look around to make sure everything in here is as it should be. Hundreds of flowers, check. Poster-sized portraits from Claire's life, check. Screen for the slideshow, check. The shiny reddish-brown casket, check.

My stomach knots. It's so archaic to have a dead body in a room that's going to be full of people. I'd have opted for an urn, which is still morbid but less so, but our dad already paid for caskets and our places in the family plot. He'd been nothing if not practical.

I take a seat on the front pew with the last of my living relatives—Mom and Ember. It hits me again that my mother really is gone—mentally—as she rambles on about an episode of *I Love Lucy*. It's hard to tell if she actually did just watch it or if she saw it many years ago.

On the other side of her, Ember looks lost in thought as she plays with a tassel on her teal dress. It had been Claire's. We'd found it in the closet when going through my sister's old room.

Just as my mom is wrapping up her summary of the show, voices sound.

I turn to them. "Sounds like people are here. Let's greet them."

Mom's dull eyes light up. "I sure hope Jack makes it. He was so nice to me when you brought me to your house."

Ember and I exchange a wide-eyed glance. We *had* brought her to the house—she hadn't recognized the place she'd lived for at least fifty years—but nobody else was there with us.

Then a chill runs through me that has nothing to do with my still-damp dress. My uncle's name had been Jack. But he'd passed away before any of us met him. His bedroom is locked on the second floor. Dad had never wanted anyone to go in and mess it up.

"Mom, how old is Jack?"

She looks deep in thought, but that doesn't mean she's thinking about my question.

More voices sound from the foyer.

I clear my throat. "We should go greet the guests."

Mom turns to Ember. "I'd say he was about your age, Lucinda."

"I'm Ember, Grandma."

Goose bumps run down my arm at my mother's words. My niece and her obsession with ghosts is getting to me. I'd take my mom's ramblings with a grain of salt, but what were the chances of her rambling about my uncle? Thinking she'd just seen him this morning?

There isn't time to worry about it. I loop my hands around their arms and lead them back toward the foyer. There is a small crowd gathered at this point. I don't recognize anyone, but that isn't surprising. I just moved back to town after being gone since I was eighteen.

We make small talk, and Ember introduces me to some of Claire's colleagues and their old neighbors. I try to keep names straight, but it isn't like I'll see most of them after today.

The door opens, and in walks a familiar face. One that makes my heart skip a beat.

Detective Graham Felton.

He had been the lead officer trying to solve my sister's murder. Since the case officially closed, we've gone on a few dates. Nothing serious—neither of us want a relationship—but I can't deny the growing attraction.

But I need to. There are too many other things to focus on, not the least of which is raising Ember. Or even just getting through this service. She's holding up rather well so far, but it's only a matter of time until she starts to fall apart. Up until this point, she's been doing a good job of keeping her mourning to herself—the occasional red splotchy skin around her eyes tells me she *is*—but funerals have a way of breaking through the roughest of exteriors.

And if she doesn't lose it, I may very well. I've been keeping myself together by staying busy and focusing on her and the house, not to mention getting back to work. But moving back home and dealing with my sister's death has brought up a lot of things I haven't wanted to deal with. It looks like life has a way of forcing you to deal with those things whether you want to or not.

Detective Felton, or Graham as I've called him on our dates, meets my gaze and gives me a slight nod.

My breath catches in my throat. I manage to nod back and hold his gaze a moment too long.

He waltzes over, weaving his way through the growing crowd of mourners. "I'm sorry about your sister." Then to Ember. "Your mom. I can't imagine the loss."

Her eyes shine with tears, and she twists a strand of her long dark hair. "Thanks."

I clear my throat. "I didn't realize you were coming, Detective." Maybe I'm being a little formal, but I don't want Ember knowing we've been seeing each other—as complicated as that is. People hire me as a fake date or friend, and the line between fake and real is becoming quickly blurred with Graham. Not only that, he was the one who helped solve Claire's murder, the one who took us seriously about it not being a suicide.

He turns back to me and gestures toward a hallway. "Can I speak with you for just a second?"

I put my hand on Ember's shoulder. "Will you be okay if I talk to him for just a moment?"

"Of course." She turns to him. "You know, whatever you say to her you can say to me. She'll tell me, anyway."

"I'll let her decide that."

Ember shrugs, then her expression lights up as she looks past me. "Gretchen's here."

"Go give her a hug."

She throws me an annoyed glance. "We're *not* huggers."

"Sorry." I hold back an amused chuckle before following Graham. "Is there news in the case? Were the trial dates set?"

"No, not yet." He glances around then lowers his voice. "The results came in from the" —he clears his throat— "*stuff* on your third floor."

"Claire's shoe?"

He shakes his head no. "That bloody knife and bedding Ember found up there."

"Oh, right." He must think I'm an idiot. "Probably nothing useful, right? It's old blood. We'll have to go through those boxes for any clues."

Graham steps closer, and my pulse races. It makes me think of dancing with him even as he's talking about a decades-old murder that took place in my house.

He pauses before speaking. "No, the lab actually did get DNA and prints."

I stare at him for a moment before finding my voice. "You know who was murdered?"

"We don't know *that* much, but we did get some interesting information."

Now he has my attention. "What?"

Graham looks around again. "Now isn't the time to get into all of that. Can I come over Monday? That way, you'll be done with all of this." He glances toward the entry, where even more people are coming in.

"You're going to make me wait two days?" I draw my brows together. "Seriously? Drop this at my sister's funeral?"

He readjusts his jacket over his ridiculously big muscles. "You're right. I'm sorry. I should've just asked if I could stop by Monday."

"Can you at least tell me something? It seems like you have something big."

He takes a deep breath. "You said your mom has memory issues?"

I nod. "Yes. She thinks her granddaughter is her sister. Why do you ask?"

Graham frowns. "Her prints were all over the knife."

"What?"

The church pastor appears, cutting off any further exchange of information. "I have a quick question before we start the service."

I give Graham my best glare before following the pastor.

2

Kenzi

I can't focus on the slideshow. In fact, I've barely been able to focus on anything said at this service.

My mom's prints are on the knife upstairs near the bloody bed. It doesn't make any sense. There was so much dust up there, and Ember said it had been completely undisturbed. That means nobody had been up there for what had to be decades.

There has to be a logical explanation. Someone could've taken one of her kitchen knives and used it while wearing gloves. She'd lived in the house for more than forty years.

Who died on the third floor so long ago? And did it have anything to do with the knife? It could've been planted. Probably was. Why else would Mom's prints be on the knife?

I glance over at her sitting next to me, watching the pictures of her daughter's life on the screen without a flicker of recognition or emotion. What secrets has her mind buried? Maybe none. The knife could just be a coincidence. The real killer might have simply grabbed the first blade they found and took it up there.

The blood was on a bed that had been used by servants over a century ago. I'd been hoping the murder had been that far in the past. But come to think of it, Graham never told me anything about the DNA. Does he know whose it was?

And now I have two whole days to think about this before he shows up to tell me anything. My mind will come up with things that are probably far more elaborate than what really happened. He's likely to tell me the DNA doesn't match anyone —and why would it? It was so long ago that whoever died wouldn't even be in the system.

The song on the slideshow switches over to something more upbeat as the pictures transition from my sister's child-hood to her teen years. She was fifteen when I was born, so we're getting closer to images and clips I actually remember. Ember insisted on putting in pictures of me, even though Claire and I were never close. She was more interested in friends than a baby sister, and she moved away to college when I was only three. We never had a chance at any real relationship.

Though maybe we could've had something if I'd stayed in town. I shove that guilt-laden thought aside just like all the rest of them. Yes, there is a lot I could've done differently, but I didn't and neither did she, and there isn't anything anybody can do to change any of it.

My focus is now on Ember. I'm taking everything I should've given my family and putting it into this girl who needs me in ways I can't begin to comprehend. It's the one thing I *can* do for my departed parents and sister. I do realize my mother is still technically here. Sitting right next to me, in fact. But the woman who always expressed her disappointment in me is gone. Claire was her golden child, and I was the royal screw-up. For her sake, I'm glad she doesn't know what's going on.

The images continue flashing on the screen. I enjoy listening to the crowd react to the photos we picked out. Now we're up to her wedding, and my skin crawls at the sight of Richard.

I hope he never again sees the outside of a prison.

Soon come the images of Claire pregnant, then of Ember as a baby.

I lean over and whisper, "You look just like her."

She shakes her head, clearly not seeing it. I get it. People have always said I look like my dad, and I don't see it. I just see me.

The slideshow ends, then one of my sister's colleagues comes up to speak. So many people have such nice things to say about her. I'm glad not everyone in her life was against her. Just two people she trusted more than any other. I clench my fists just thinking about them.

A couple of her friends from school speak, the pastor gives some closing thoughts, and then it's over. The service, anyway. There is still a lot to do before we can head back home and collapse.

Ember and I help Mom stand, then the three of us make our way back to the foyer and line up to receive condolences and speak with the guests. My mother does a good job of interacting with people. Other than the fact that she didn't use anyone's names when speaking with them, it would almost be impossible to know the true state of her mind.

The sanctuary empties, and I glance around for Graham. I'm still annoyed with him, but I also want to see him again before he leaves.

The pastor invites everyone to go downstairs for food and fellowship.

Ember and I help Mom down the stairs and into a seat at a table. I ask her what she wants to eat, and she replies with a story about a checkers match with someone at the home.

"I'll find something you like. Stay here."

She picks up a napkin. "It was so nice that Jack made it to the service, don't you think?"

I give her a double-take. "What did you say?"

"Jack. He's such a nice boy."

Blood drains from my face as I exchange a worried glance with Ember. "Maybe you should stay here with her."

"Okay." She sits.

I struggle to take a deep breath as I make my way to the food table. Really, I shouldn't let her words get to me. It's just the ramblings of a woman who can't make sense of her memories. But my uncle wasn't someone she ever would have met.

It's just plain creepy.

Unless she's confusing her memories of Dad with his brother. Relief washes through me at that thought. Sure, it's a stretch, but so is making sense of how her mind works. She must be recalling times with Dad when they were young and childless. Still not sure why she'd call him by his deceased brother's name, but she's clearly somehow confused the two men. That's the only thing that makes sense.

I'm either good at weaving wild tales or I'm the memory whisperer. Doesn't matter. As long as I stop thinking a ghost resides in my house.

As I stand in line dishing up food for Mom and me, I look around for the detective. The man seems to have disappeared. But what do I expect after glaring at him the way I did?

Near the end of the table, a few girls about Ember's age are gathered together. I'm trying to figure out if they're her friends or just kids of other guests when part of their conversation drifts my way.

"Everyone says it's a haunted house."

"I heard about lights turning on when nobody's home, even when it's not Halloween."

"My mom says there used to be science experiments in the basement—done on people!"

I bite back the urge to tell them to keep quiet and take the plates over to the table. Ember is sitting with Gretchen, and they're sharing a plate of food.

Mom picks up a miniature sandwich from the plate I've slipped in front of her then starts talking about a friend who passed away years earlier.

I stay half-engaged, my attention divided between her and looking around for Graham again. He's nowhere to be seen, but one of the other officers is sitting near the back.

He's staring at my mom.

They can't seriously be looking at her as a suspect? The woman has no real memories of the past, much less of any crime she might have been framed for.

I take a deep breath and march over to him.

He glances up at me, his expression surprised. "Is everything okay, Miss Brannon?"

"I'm looking for Detective Felton."

"He was called out during the service. Said he'd stop by your house on Monday."

"When was he called out?"

"During one of the songs. Just before the slideshow. Why?"

I shrug. "Just asking."

His gaze drifts back to my mom.

"You do realize she can't remember anything?"

The officer turns back to me. "Pardon me?"

"My mother. You keep looking at her."

He doesn't deny it.

"She thinks she's living in an episode of *I Love Lucy*. You'd be better off focusing on real criminals." I don't give him a chance to respond before walking away.

It takes me forever to get through my plate of food because people keep stopping over to speak with us. I don't blame them, but my stomach is rumbling and I need sustenance. It's been such a long day. I'm definitely looking forward to going home. Ember and I will probably crash on a couch and stream a movie while eating flavored popcorn. Doing that has turned into our thing.

After the room empties, Mom turns to me. "Are we going back to your house? I'd like to see Jack again. He's such a nice boy."

"You've mentioned that." I exchange a look with Ember.

Mom's expression lights up. "I can come with you?"

I check the time. "We're supposed to return you to your home soon. You only have a day pass, not a night pass."

She frowns. "Can I come back soon? Will you bring me?"

Guilt stings. She's probably been super lonely in that home. "I'll speak with the person in charge."

"I'd love to visit. Maybe even stay a while."

My stomach knots. "I'm not sure about that, Mom."

She blinks a few times. "Why not?"

"They have rules." How do I explain to her that she's there for a reason? That Ember and I aren't able to meet her needs. We couldn't leave her alone at the house, and I can't watch her all the time. Ember will be starting school before long, and we both work in the evenings for the most part.

Mom remains quiet as the pastor helps us gather the things into my car.

As we near the retirement home, Mom turns to me. "I remember the day Claire was born."

"You do?"

"The happiest day of my life."

"That's great." Thanks, Mom. What about the day I was born?

Obviously, I'm not that memorable. At least not to my mother.

3

Ember

I flop onto my bed and close my eyes, every muscle aching. The stress didn't hit me until we got home. Obviously, my mom's funeral was horribly emotional. I mean, seriously, who expects that at fifteen? I have enough to deal with as it is without adding my mom's murder to everything.

It's no wonder my aunt keeps bringing up the idea of counseling. But I don't want to unload everything to some stranger, no matter what kind of training she's had. I can deal with it myself just fine. So far, so good.

Thank God I have a best friend who knows me. Gretchen wrapped her arms around me even though we aren't the touchy-feely type. She made fun of the mean girls who were there to make me feel better. I don't know if that makes us awful or not, but it felt a lot better than having to talk to them. Maybe one day I'll be ready to face them, but today is not that day.

Bump, bump.

I jolt at the noise. It's probably just Kenzi getting ready for bed. But this enormous house makes all kinds of sounds, especially at night. Thumps, bumps, knocks, scratches—you name it.

It doesn't help that our house is the subject of so many rumors. The cute guy who delivers our groceries always tells me stories. At first, he was nervous, thinking my aunt would get him fired, but since I never told her anything he said, he's come to trust me.

It's hard to say how much is true, but from how many stories Luke's told me, it's hard to believe they're all rumors. And he doesn't even know about the ancient murder scene I discovered on the third floor. The police took the knife and bedding—going as far as to cut out the bloody part of the mattress. My guess is they'll never solve the murder. If one of the servants killed another, that would've had to be over a hundred years ago.

Kenzi and I will have to eventually go through the boxes upstairs to figure anything out. But our main focus is on the first two levels while we continue to settle in. And given how many people today expressed interest in visiting us, we not only have to keep working on that, we need to work faster. There are still a lot of things covered in sheets and rooms we haven't gone into yet.

Like Jack's room.

A chill runs down my spine thinking of that. It was driving me crazy when Grandma kept talking about seeing him. She never once met him if Grandpa's stories are true. Family history indicates he would have died before they were adults.

My great-uncle's room is actually next door to mine. This was Kenzi's room growing up, and now it's mine. She has Grandma and Grandpa's old room.

I wish my mind would shut up. The last thing I want to think about is any of this. I just want a normal life. But that isn't going to happen. Not when I live in the Brannon House, a local legend that literally goes bump in the night.

What else can I think of? There has to be something else.

Actually, there is.

The letter that I've been ignoring. It's from my mom, and in it she told me everything she knows about my birth father. I haven't told anyone about it.

Now that I have the information I need to find him, I'm paralyzed. There are too many what-ifs. He probably has a family of his own by now and doesn't want it interrupted by a surprise child. His wife will likely despise me. So will his other kids.

On the other hand, he might actually be happy by the news. It's not like he knew about me and ran off. He and Mom had one night together and went their separate ways across the country from each other. And that leads me to my greatest worry.

If he actually wants me in his life, he might be able to take me away. I don't want to live on the east coast. Don't want to leave my friends or my school, even though most of the kids are jerks. I'd rather take my chances with Kenzi and this potentially haunted house than whatever unknown lies clear across the country.

Better the devil you know than the one you don't, or whatever that saying is. Not that my aunt is evil—she's surprisingly cool. It's just my life has fallen apart and I'm just starting to rebuild. I don't want to have everything ripped from me again. And a birth father might be able to make that happen.

His name is Graham. The other name from the letter is Sasha Beckett—Mom's friend who took her to the party. Those names are burned into my mind now. The question is, will I ever do anything with that information?

Bump, bump, scratch!

What if Kenzi's moving something heavy again? I better see if she needs help before she hurts herself.

I force myself off the bed, my muscles protesting, and I open the door.

Everything is dark except the faint glow coming from the nightlights every fifty feet or so between here and the bathroom, which is closer to Kenzi's room than mine even though she has a private bathroom. Some things in this house make no sense.

I shut the door as quietly as possible. If there *are* ghosts, I don't want them to know I heard them. My hope is that if I act like I don't believe, they'll leave me alone. Kenzi says the house is just settling, and she hasn't heard anything unusual. Or if she has, she hasn't told me.

Goose bumps form on my arm. Why do I do this to myself?

I jump into bed without changing into my pajamas and pull the covers up over my head. You know, because *that* will protect me from a malicious spirit.

4

Kenzi

It's Monday, and Graham is already five minutes late. I pace the kitchen, looking out the window each time I pass it. Given his job, running late seems to be par for the course. He runs into life-or-death situations every day, and coming here to discuss a decades-old crime is the least of his concerns.

I'm glad Ember is helping out at a kids' art camp this week. It not only gives me the space to talk freely about this with Graham before telling her about it, but the job will also help her get her mind off everything. I heard her sobbing when I got up for a midnight snack. She ignored my knocking and asking if she was okay. Then this morning, she acted like nothing happened. Seems to be how she's dealing with things—on her own. Maybe I can get her to open up with ice cream later.

Ding-dong!

I stop my pacing and mosey to the door. He made me wait all weekend to hear what he found, so he can wait a minute as I make my way to the entry.

When I open the door, he gives me a big grin and pushes off

his aviators, balancing two coffees. "Sorry I'm late. I stopped to pick up lattes."

My mouth falls open. He stopped to pick me up coffee? Well, us. Graham picked up one for him and one for me. Probably from a stand on the way. They're all over. It's no big deal.

He holds out one toward me, still smiling.

"Thanks." I take it. "You didn't have to."

"Peace offering." He steps inside. "Kitchen?"

"Sure." I lead the way. "This is a peace offering?"

"You weren't very happy with me at the service for not telling you everything. And you were right, I shouldn't have said anything other than the fact that we needed to talk."

I sip the latte. It has a hint of caramel and the corners of my mouth twitch. He really is sorry. "Nobody's perfect. I say things I shouldn't all the time." Like the time I invited him on a date when he was investigating my sister's death. If anyone should understand a running mouth, it's me. "Are you hungry? I have donuts."

He lifts a brow. "You saying that because I'm a cop, I automatically like donuts?"

"No!" My face warms. "Ember likes them, so I picked some up. Actually, now you can't have any."

Graham laughs. "That's too bad. I love donuts."

"Too late."

He looks at me like he can't tell if I'm serious or not.

"Plain yogurt for you." I open the fridge and look around.

"I'll stick with the latte, thanks."

I turn around, grab the donut box from the counter, and take it to the table. "I'm totally kidding. Eat."

We make some small talk for a few minutes while we eat and drink our daily intake of sugar.

Then he leans back and takes a deep breath. "So, you probably want to know about the knife."

A door slams upstairs.

He glances toward the hallway. "Is Ember mad?"

"No, she's not here. I have some windows open, and it doesn't take much of a breeze for some of them to open and close."

"You don't find that unnerving?" He turns back to me.

"Why? Because this is the legendary Brannon House?"

He doesn't answer the question. Instead pulls out his phone and looks at it for a moment.

"What did you find from the bedding and knife?"

"I already told you about the prints." He's still looking at the screen.

"Yes, and that makes complete sense given that my mom lived here for over forty years. She and my dad were the last ones to go up there that I know about."

The detective looks up at me, his mouth in a straight line. "But that doesn't explain the DNA."

"What about it?" My voice catches, not allowing me to say more.

He holds my gaze for a moment. "It belongs to a relative of yours."

The words are like a slap to the face.

"You don't happen to know of any relatives whose blood that might be?"

"One ... one of my relatives? The blood belongs to a family member?" My mind swims, trying to make sense of the news.

Graham nods. "Do you know of anyone who died here? Or was seriously injured? I couldn't find anything in the city records."

I take a few slow breaths to give myself a moment to gather my thoughts. Then I look him in the eyes. "How do you know it belongs to one of my relatives?"

"DNA can trace familial lines."

"I know that! But I'm not on file, and I can't imagine why my parents or sister would be either."

"Yours is on file. That's how I know the blood belongs to someone in your family line."

The room spins around me. I reach for the table to steady myself and nearly knock over my latte.

He reaches over and grabs it before it falls. "Are you okay?"

"Why is my DNA on file?"

"The reason is sealed. You must've been a minor."

"Obviously," I mutter.

Graham rests his hand on mine. "I'm sorry for upsetting you. Maybe I should talk to another of your relatives."

"Who? Ember will know less than me—she's only fifteen. And my mom has dementia. I'm all you've got."

"What about your brother?"

"My *brother*?"

Graham nods, his hand still on mine. "He might be the key to the answers."

"I don't *have* a brother!"

"Is he dead too?"

I stare at the detective. "No. I don't have a brother. It was just Claire and me."

His brows draw together and his expression tightens, but I can't tell what he's thinking.

"What's going on?"

"There's a birth certificate for a son born to your parents ten years before your sister."

I struggle to breathe, to keep my balance. "You're wrong."

He shakes his head. "I'm sorry. Are you okay? Do you need to lie down?"

"No." I don't know which question I'm answering. "What's the name?"

"Of what?"

"On the birth certificate!"

"I believe it was Jack."

Jack. The same name my mom kept mentioning at the service. She kept seeing Jack all day.

Had she been talking about her son? Not my uncle?

"No!" This is ridiculous.

"No?" Graham asks. "His name wasn't Jack?"

"I don't have a brother! My parents didn't have another child. They would have told me!" Hot, angry tears sting my eyes.

Did my parents lie to me my entire life? Did Claire know about our brother? Did everyone? Did Ember?

Graham squeezes my hand.

I jolt, realizing we're still touching. He becomes blurry as tears well in my eyes. I blink, and two fat drops spill out.

He scoots the chair over and wraps his arms around me, pressing me against his chest. His racing heart thumps against my ear. "I'm sorry, Kenzi. I didn't realize this would be news to you."

I nod my head and try to stop the tears.

My parents had a son and never told me. Not one mention, ever. I'd have remembered something like that.

I struggle to take in deep breaths and make sense of the news. If he was ten years older than Claire, that would make him twenty-five years older than me. I'd have easily never met him. What if they had a falling out, and cut him out of their lives? That would mean my sister would've known him and purposefully never told me about him.

What about that room upstairs? It was supposed to belong to my dad's brother. My uncle, Jack. What if it actually belonged to my brother?

"Kenzi?"

I pull back and look at Graham, not caring that my makeup is probably a mess.

"We can talk about this later. Once you've had some time to process everything."

"That could be a while." I tuck some hair behind an ear. "I can't imagine coming to terms with this any time soon."

He nods. "So, you don't know how to contact your brother?"

"What if that's his blood up there? How would you find out?"

"It's not."

"How do you know?" My tone is more accusatory than I mean it to be.

"Because it isn't close enough to be a sibling's or parent's, but it *is* a relative's."

"Like an uncle?"

He nods. "Could be an uncle. Or nephew or cousin. Someone outside your direct family."

"You only mention male relatives. It's definitely a guy's blood?"

"Yes."

"Was there enough to confirm someone actually died?"

Graham shakes his head. "Not on the bed. But if there was a pool of it on the floor that had been cleaned, I'd say yes. Definitely enough to kill a person."

A lump forms in my throat, and I fight more angry tears. "How do I go about finding my brother?"

If he's alive.

"I can start an investigation. Check to see if he's ever been on a missing persons list. There are a lot of options, but it'll take time."

"There's no death certificate?"

He shakes his head no and says more.

But I can't focus on what he's saying. Pressure is building behind my temples. "You know what? I think I do need to lie down."

"Do you want me to help you up the stairs?"

"No. I can get up there myself."

He rises, and I walk him to the front door. Or he walks me, I'm not really sure.

We say a few words before he leaves. I have no idea what, though.

Now I'm alone in this enormous house full of secrets. Lies. Deception.

What really happened here? If only the walls could talk. I'd take one of Ember's imaginary ghosts at this point.

A door slams shut upstairs.

The first thing I need to do is close the windows. I could use the fresh air, but there seems to be no way to stop the doors from opening and closing with the breezes.

I lean on the ornate railing, remembering leaping up the stairs as a child. Innocent and carefree, never imagining the secrets held by this house and my loved ones.

When I reach the landing, I look over toward the door to the third floor.

I have to go through those old boxes sooner than I'd planned.

5

Ember

My aunt has hardly said two words through dinner. Usually, she talks my ear off. Not that I'm complaining, but something is definitely wrong. And so far, nothing I've said has gotten her to open up.

"Did somebody else die?"

Her eyes widen. "What?"

"You're acting weird. If you have bad news, just tell me. I can handle it."

She chews on her lower lip and twists her long hair into a bun, wrapping it in a scrunchy from her wrist. "Let's talk after dinner."

"Okay. Are you even eating?"

Kenzi looks down at her barely-touched food and sighs. "I don't have much of an appetite right now."

"Wait. Aren't you supposed to be working now?"

"I canceled."

That confirms it—something is definitely wrong. She hasn't

missed a job since she started working up here. My stomach knots, and now I don't want to finish my food.

"Eat." She motions toward my plate.

"After you." I lean back and cross my arms.

She tilts her head.

I don't budge.

"Why don't we go for a walk?" she asks. "I could use some air."

"Sure."

We don't bother putting anything away. Instead of heading for the front door, she goes for the back.

"The backyard?" I ask.

She nods and keeps walking. We pass my grandpa's old office. Papers are spread out on the floor.

"What happened in there?"

"I'm going through his files."

"At least it wasn't a ghost."

My aunt throws me an exasperated look. "Would you stop? All those noises we heard before were just Richard trying to scare us. That's much creepier than a spirit, anyway."

She may be right, but that doesn't explain all the sounds I've been hearing since Richard's arrest. I keep that thought to myself for the time being. "What are you looking for?"

"Records."

"What kind?"

"We'll discuss it outside."

"Don't want the ghosts to hear?"

She gives me another glance.

We pass the library. "You know, years ago people kept records in books. Grandpa once showed me some scrawlings in a book there. I think it was a family tree? I was only five or six, so I'm not entirely sure. But maybe you'll find something in one of those books."

Kenzi hesitates. "I hadn't thought of that. Good idea."

We make our way outside, where the grass goes past our ankles.

She locks the door, sighs, and pulls out her phone. "I'd better add lawn service to my ever-growing to-do list."

"Are you okay? You really aren't acting like yourself. I miss bubbly Kenzi."

Her expression contorts into a scowl. "You'll understand soon enough."

My stomach knots again. Now I'm not sure I want to know.

We walk the length of the main part of the yard, and she keeps going once we reach the woods.

"We're going in there?" My heart picks up speed, and I can almost hear Grandpa warning me to never go into the woods.

My aunt glances at me and nods. "There's something I need to see."

I swallow. "If you say so."

We step into the darkness. All I can think about is that this was where Richard came and went when sneaking into the house.

Strange noises sound in the distance. It has to be animals, but that doesn't stop goose bumps from forming on my arm. I don't recognize any of the sounds.

And Kenzi isn't any help. She says nothing as she marches on, weaving around trees and bushes.

"Have you been in here before?"

She simply nods.

"So, you know where we're going? Not just tromping around at random?"

"Let me think."

It's my turn to sigh. As long as we don't run into any rabid animals or axe murderers, I won't complain. Or ghosts. This place is just as creepy as the house was when we first moved in —after everything had been mostly untouched for the last five years.

Just when I'm nearly convinced we've reached the edge of the earth, we come to a clearing. The grass is even longer than in the yard, and colorful wildflowers decorate the landscape.

I can scarcely breathe. "Is this still our property?"

"Yeah. Come over here." She leads me to the left. Tucked behind a copse of trees is a small iron gate with points on the top.

It protects gravestones.

I gasp.

She turns to me. "The original family plot."

The tiny hairs on the back of my neck stand on end. I look around to see if anyone is watching us but no one's there. Not anyone alive, anyway.

"Our family was the first to settle in the area," she explains. "There was no cemetery until others moved in. Everyone was buried here until my great-grandparents—your great-great-grandparents—decided to reserve a plot in town."

I have no words.

She points past the fence. "And over there is where the servants were laid to rest."

"Where?"

"Just the land. They didn't get fencing or grave markers."

I picture their tiny rooms on the third floor and anger bubbles. "Why were they treated so poorly? It's like they were less than human or something! Those terrible living quarters. Having to eat in the pantry after everyone else. I hate that the people who treated them so badly are in our bloodline! I wish it were the other way."

"We can't help what our ancestors did."

I squeeze my fists. "I wish I could."

She opens the gate. It squeaks and squeals in protest. "Want to come in?"

"Can I give them a piece of my mind?"

"Sure."

I march in, glowering at the stones. Then my anger melts away as I see some of the dates. Some of these people were only children.

My aunt wanders around the fence line, looking at the ground rather than the graves. I nearly ask her what she's doing, but my curiosity about the headstones gets the best of me. I have to clear moss and dirt to read some of the etchings. Then I snap pictures. Gretchen is never going to believe this. I barely can, and I'm standing here. How could these have been here my whole life and nobody ever told me? Was this why my grandparents never wanted me to go into the woods? Or did they just not want to deal with chasing after me in their old age?

Kenzi passes me, still focused on the outer edge of the tiny cemetery.

"What are you looking for?"

She turns to me, her eyes shining. "An unmarked grave."

"Whose?"

"Jack's." She closes her eyes for a few moments before opening them and clearing her throat.

"But wouldn't Grandpa's brother be in the family plot in town? Not this one?"

"Have a seat." She points to a metal bench covered in moss that looks like it could fall apart if I glance at it wrong.

"Um ..."

"It's sturdy." She yanks off moss, pulls out a small towel from her handbag, and wipes the seat.

"You were ready to clean that off?"

"Yeah." She plops down. "See? Sturdy."

I study it for a moment and finally sit. It doesn't so much as creak.

"Why would Jack be buried here?"

"There's another Jack in our family."

"Huh?" I try to make sense of what she means. "Like, Grandpa's brother was named after someone?"

She draws in a deep breath. "Detective Felton came by today with some news on that knife and bed you found on the third floor."

"You're confusing me. What does this have to do with anything?"

"He told me there's a record showing you have an uncle named Jack."

"*I* have an uncle?"

Kenzi tugs on her bun. "Did your mom ever mention having an older brother?"

"What?" I exclaim. "No, never."

Her expression tightens. "She either didn't know or never spoke about him."

"Apparently. Are you sure about that?"

She looks out over the gravestones before speaking. "The detective is certain. There's a birth certificate but no death certificate."

Everything starts to make sense. "You think he was buried here?"

"Maybe. But if he was, his resting place wasn't marked. And it's been too long to tell where he would've been placed."

I leap to my feet. "Was it his blood up there?"

She shakes her head. "No, but it was a relative."

"How do they know it wasn't his?"

"The DNA shows it isn't close enough of a relative to be one of my siblings."

"Oh." I sit back down and look at the stones of our ancestors. "So, maybe the blood was one of theirs."

"Maybe." She doesn't sound like she believes it.

"What aren't you telling me?"

"I don't think it means anything."

"What doesn't?" I ask. "Don't hold back on me."

My aunt holds my gaze for a moment. "Your grandma's prints were on the knife."

"Are you saying Grandma killed someone? Grandma?"

She shakes her head. "She lived here. Someone could've grabbed that knife from the kitchen and used it while wearing gloves. It doesn't prove a thing."

Silence rests between us as I try to connect the dots. I have an uncle, maybe alive and maybe dead. And my memory-compromised grandmother is possibly implicated in the murder of another relative.

I turn to Kenzi. "Which Jack was Grandma talking about on Saturday?"

"I don't know, but we need to find out."

6

Kenzi

I pull into the parking spot and turn to Ember. "Are you ready?"

She glances over at the retirement center. "You think she'll remember anything?"

"There's only one way to find out." I pull down my visor and check my reflection in the mirror before getting out.

Ember plays with her hair as we make our way to the front door. After I press the button, the receptionist unlocks the door from her seat. She's the same person we saw on Saturday when picking up Mom for the service.

"Back again for Regina? She'll be so happy."

"I sure hope so. We're good for another field trip?"

She chuckles. "She's having a great day. Perfect timing for a short outing."

I clear my throat. "What about a night pass?"

"You mean overnight?"

"Yeah. It's already late afternoon."

The girl flips through some papers. "Well, that's a whole

different matter. I'm not sure about that. You'd have to speak with her head nurse."

I lift a brow. "You can okay a day pass, but not an overnighter?"

"Regina's already approved for day passes with you. She's been doing so much better since returning after the memorial. Even though it was a sad occasion, it did her a world of good to be with family."

"Wouldn't a night at the house she lived in for over forty years be even better?"

She shifts her weight. "Like I said, you'll have to talk with her head nurse."

Annoyance runs through me. They're treating her like a prisoner. I force a smile. "Put her down for the day pass, and I'll see what I can do about an overnighter."

"Sure thing." She clacks on her keyboard.

We walk down the hall toward Mom's room, and I smile at everyone we pass. We don't come across any nurses.

Ember turns to me. "Why do they make it so hard to get her out? You'd think they'd be happy for a break."

I shrug. "Who knows? I'm sure they have their reasons, but they act like she's not paying them to stay here. This isn't a prison or mental facility."

In the room, Mom is sitting on her couch watching a black-and-white show I don't recognize.

She turns to us, not showing recognition at first. Then her expression lights up. "Doris! Jane! You came again. Have a seat."

Ember steps closer. "Actually, Grandma, we're here to bring you home. Remember going there two days ago?"

"Will Jack be there? He's such a nice boy."

Ember glances at me.

I smile at Mom. "He might be. Do you want to come with us and see?"

"Yes. Let's wait until my show is over."

"It's getting close to dinnertime. We should get going sooner rather than later."

Ember steps closer. "Maybe waiting will give you time to find the head nurse."

"That's true." I turn to Mom. "Ember's going to watch with you while I ask your nurse a question."

"Thanks," Ember mutters.

Mom turns back to her show.

"You'll be fine. Just talk to her like the characters are here in the room, and you'll be okay."

She nods and takes a seat while I go back into the empty hallway. Mom's room is at the far end, away from the nurses' station, which is usually noisy and bustling. I make my way there.

One of the nurses tells me the head nurse is at the other end of the building.

Of course she is. I make my way to the opposite side of the wing, glancing in the open doors for the woman. Just as I'm about to give up, she steps out from behind a closed door.

The older woman's eyes light up. "You're here to see Regina again!"

"I am, and I have a question about that."

"Is she doing okay? She's been in such a great mood since you took her out the other day."

"That's what I want to talk about, actually."

She nods for me to keep going.

"My mom really improved after spending time at the house. She doesn't remember living there for nearly five decades, but it did jog memories. Some of what she said was right."

The nurse smiles. "Is that where you're going to take her? I saw she has a day pass."

"I'd like for her to spend the night with us."

She jolts. "You would?"

"Yes. What if we're able to bring back more of her memories? Her personality?"

"We need to take this one step at a time. Another day pass is a fantastic idea. Let's do that a few more times to make sure she reacts consistently. Then we can discuss an overnight pass."

"What's the problem? That's her real home. Ember and I are her family."

"I understand that. But do you know how to take care of someone with such advanced dementia?"

I straighten my back. "We did great the other day."

"That was a few hours. You didn't have to give her any medicine or get her into bed."

"I'm sure I could handle giving my mother some medication and helping her into bed."

"Do you have a bed with a railing? She's been prone to falling."

"I could get something."

She adjusts her collar. "And what if she has a breakdown? Do you have a plan for that? If she shouts and throws things?"

"I grew up with her. I'm sure I can figure it out."

"Let's talk after today's outing."

"I can handle my own mother!" I narrow my eyes.

"Is that why you moved to California?" She lifts a brow.

"Excuse me?" I exclaim. "I moved there because I became an adult and wanted a different experience—not that it's any of your business."

"All I'm saying is family dynamics are often complicated. And she was likely to have already experienced early symptoms back then, though you didn't realize it. As a teenager, you probably viewed it as typical mother-daughter angst. Let's give today a try, then we can discuss the possibility of a longer visit. Maybe an all-day one—morning to night. A few hours is different from overnight."

"Does that cut into the facility's pay? Is that what this is about?"

The nurse tilts her head. "No. It's about patient *safety*. We have regulations in place for a reason." She glances at a sheet of paper. "I need to check on another patient. Have a nice visit with your mother."

She takes off before I can say another word.

I need to look into typical protocols and find out if this is normal. Claire and Richard moved Mom in here after my dad died, and I could see Richard setting up something formal regarding the length and time of Mom's passes so he wouldn't have to deal with her visiting his place.

When I get back to her room, Ember jumps up from the couch. "Are we leaving? Is she staying overnight?"

"Not yet. Has she said anything about what we discussed?"

She glances at Mom, who's still watching the TV, and shakes her head. "Nothing other than her show."

I take a deep breath. "Being at home will help. Even if it ends up being a slower process than we'd like."

While we're getting her ready to go, a nurse comes in and goes over the details of the day pass with us, emphasizing the time Mom needs to come back. I push aside my irritation and stay friendly.

I can't help but feel like Richard is somehow pulling strings, even from behind bars.

Finally, we're in the car heading home. I pick up some takeout on the way, so we don't lose any valuable time cooking. Ember and I need to spend as much of the visit as possible trying to jog Mom's memories. It's not like I expect her to spill the story about the knife today, but if we can make a little more progress than last time, maybe we can get closer to unearthing that story. She did bring up Jack again.

Maybe she'd even remember the truth about the son she never mentioned to me.

7

Kenzi

I dump the last of the chicken fried rice into a bowl and sit at the kitchen table. Mom chose the seat she always sat at when I was growing up. I also picked my usual chair. But all my memories are intact.

Could she remember more than she's letting on? There's certainly a lot she has reason to hide. How many people need to keep a child and possible murder secret?

Mom grabs her wrist, the wrinkles around her eyes deepening. "My bracelet! It's gone!"

I hold back a groan. "Is it the same one you lost in the car on Saturday?"

"Oh, I never take it off."

"I'll check the car after we eat." I pick up my fork.

She holds out her arm and rubs her wrist quickly. "I can't do anything without my bracelet."

I place my fork onto the plate. "I'll get it. It's no trouble at all."

Her expression relaxes. "Thank you, Doris."

"I thought Ember was Doris," I mumble.

"What was that?"

"Nothing." I push my chair back and force a smile. "I'll be right back."

If it's going to be like this, maybe it's a good thing we didn't get approved for the overnighter. I have no desire to chase down her jewelry constantly. If she loses it in this house, she's straight up out of luck. I'm not turning this place upside down.

Outside, I lean against the door, take a deep breath, and let the sun's warm rays relax me. Once I've calmed a bit, I go to the Mercedes and check the passenger seat. The bracelet is exactly where it was when I had to run through the pouring rain to find it.

I lock the car and wave to a well-dressed man, probably in his forties, walking his dog.

He nods at me and walks over. "Hello, neighbor."

I clear my throat. "Uh, hi. You live around here?"

The dude nods again and adjusts the collar of his shirt. "Two doors down. Name's Dustin Wells. You are?"

"Kenzi Brannon." I hold out my hand.

"Brannon?" He shakes, his grip firm. "You're related to the original family."

"Yeah. I grew up here, actually." I don't know why I feel the need to explain anything to him. I can't even tell if he's being genuinely neighborly or not.

He smiles, showing off his pearly whites. Straight and bright. A little too perfect. "It's staying in the family. That's wonderful news."

"It has since it was built." I pull my hand from his grip.

"Really?" He turns his attention to the house. "Is it true it's the oldest home on the street?"

"That's right. The first in town, if I remember correctly. I need to brush up on my house's history."

Dustin scratches his chin, still looking at my home. "It's

over a hundred years old, isn't it?"

"Maybe closer to two." I try to remember all the things my parents told me growing up, but I never took any interest back then. Now I wish I'd paid more attention. I hadn't expected Dad to pass away so soon after I left or for Mom to forget everything. But I did know they were getting up there in years. It shouldn't have surprised me.

"Two centuries?" Dustin looks at me, his smile fading. "I hadn't realized it was so old. Was your family one of the first in the state?"

I shrug. "No idea. Looks like I'm going to have to do even more digging than I thought." I glance at the house, trying to see in the kitchen window. I can't. "It was nice meeting you. I need to get back inside."

"Of course. If you want any help looking into the past events of the place, just let me know. I'm somewhat of a history buff, and this place has held my interest since my wife and I moved in."

"What's so interesting about it?" I stare at the house, not seeing anything other than the place I grew up, now looking run down and sad—as if an inanimate object could actually have emotions.

"It's the oldest one on the street, and people talk. Seems there are more rumors than facts to be found."

"It's just a house." I throw him a questioning glance.

He nods enthusiastically. "It's the oldest in the area! There are so many stories. I'm so curious to know how many are true."

This guy seems odd. "Where did you say you live again?"

He points down the street. "Two houses that way."

"Is it your family house too?"

Dustin shakes his head. "No. We bought it and moved in just over five years ago."

That explains the questions. He never would have met my parents, who'd have gladly told him everything they knew about the house. They loved telling the stories to anyone who would listen.

"I'd better get inside." I step away from him. "I'll see you around."

He starts to say something, but I hurry away and wave, not wanting to get sucked into more conversation. I'd already told him I needed to go, yet he'd kept talking about the house.

When I return to the kitchen, my niece and mother are nearly done eating.

"Here's your bracelet." I hand it to her. "Exactly where it was the other day. You'll have to be more careful with that if you don't want to lose it."

"Oh, thank you. I don't know what I'd do without it." She struggles with the clasp before sliding it on. "Can I walk around the house? It's such a lovely home."

I glance at my full plate. "It'll only take me a few minutes to eat."

"Take your time, Jane. I'll just wander around myself."

Like that's going to happen. I turn to Ember. "Stay with your grandmother. I'll catch up in a few."

She nods, takes a few bites, then helps Mom up.

"Really, I don't want to be a bother. You don't have to babysit me. I'm an old woman, not an imbecile."

Ember throws me a pleading glance.

I smile at my mom. "We want to spend time with you. That's why we brought you here."

"We both know that's not true, dear. I've been wasting away in that room for years without a single visitor."

And there it is—the guilt trip. Even without her memories, that part of her is still there. How long until she reminds me what a disappointment I am? At least that would give me an opening to ask about my brother.

"Ember and Claire visited you plenty of times, Mom."

She gives me an icy stare. "You didn't."

A chill runs down my back, and I nearly drop my fork. "I was in LA, but I'm back now. Enjoy walking around. Maybe something will bring back some happy memories."

Mom turns around and takes slow steps out to the hall.

Ember holds one of her arms and gives me another desperate look.

"I'll hurry." I stuff some rice into my mouth and scarf the food down as quickly as I can. With each passing minute, I'm growing more relieved about not having Mom spend the night. She hasn't mentioned anything useful yet, and she's getting under my skin in the same ways that originally sent me running to another state.

I finish my food then hurry into the hall without putting anything away. That can wait. We don't have much time to try and pull memories from her before returning her to the retirement home.

She and Ember are in Dad's office. Mom is sitting at the desk, looking through a drawer.

I step close to my niece and whisper, "How's it going?"

Ember shrugs. "She wanted to come in here. I tried to get her to go upstairs. Thought it'd be interesting for her to pass Jack's room."

"I'd like to see her reaction to that."

"Or the door to the third floor."

I nod. "Did she say anything interesting?"

"Not really. She talked about that show she was watching before insisting we come in here."

"What do you make of the bracelet that keeps going missing?"

"I guess she likes it."

"It seems to me she's using it to get rid of me."

Ember's forehead wrinkles. "You think so?"

"It wouldn't surprise me. What did she talk about while I was outside?"

"Nothing really. She complained about not liking Chinese food."

"Seriously? That was her idea."

"Yep."

I draw in a deep breath before stepping closer to the desk. "Are you looking for something, Mom?"

She doesn't glance up. "We're trying to bring back my memories, aren't we? You say I used to live here. Maybe this desk has something. It seems important."

"This was Dad's office. You never really came in here."

"Didn't I?" She closes the drawer and opens another.

"Are you sure you're not looking for something?"

"My memories."

"There are plenty of other rooms that will help with that."

No response. She keeps going through Dad's things.

"Jack has a room upstairs."

She looks up at me, her face paling. "Pardon?"

"Jack."

"Oh, yes." She tugs on a curl. "He's such a nice boy."

"Maybe he's in his room. What do you think?"

Mom clears her throat. "This is your house. Wouldn't you know if he's here?"

"He comes and goes as he pleases."

Her only response is to look away and pick up a framed photo of her and Dad at their wedding.

I try to prompt her toward the answers I want. "That's how Jack rolls. You know how brothers are."

She drops the picture. It hits the desk, then the wooden arm of the chair, and finally the hardwood floor. The glass shatters.

"Look what you've done!" Mom's wrinkled brows draw together as she turns to me. "What a mess!"

My heart hammers as I walk around the massive desk. "I'll clean that later." I help her up. "Let's get out of here for now."

"That picture! It's ruined! You destroyed it!"

"Only the glass is broken." I bend down and pick up the photo, careful not to cut myself on the glass shards. "See? Not a scratch."

Her nostrils flare. "It could've been ruined!"

"There are other copies, Mom. It would've been perfectly fine even if something had happened to this one."

"You'd like that, wouldn't you?" She hits my hand away.

"Mom!"

"Leave me alone! Go away!"

I step back away from her reach. "It wouldn't be safe to leave you alone."

"Then leave me with the girl."

Ember whips her head toward me, eyes wide.

I count to ten silently. "No. I need you to relax, or we're going to have to take you back to your room."

Her stance relaxes. "My room? The room here? You'd take me upstairs?"

"Ember already offered. Yes, we'll take you there."

"She did no such thing." Mom crosses her arms.

Ember's mouth drops open. "Yes, I did! You wanted to come in here."

My mother screams. It's an ear-piercing sound, scarcely possible from such a frail woman.

"Mom!" I put my hand on her arm.

She swings at me, still hollering.

Ember runs out of the room.

"Stop!" I put both my hands on her shoulders and hold her gaze.

She quits her yelling.

My ears ring. "Do you want to be able to come back here again?"

Her mouth forms a straight line.

"Do you?"

"Yes."

I step even closer, glass crunching under my shoes. "Then you can't act like this. Do you understand? I spoke to your head nurse about possibly having you spend a night here, but that will never happen if you treat us like this."

She steps back, bumps into the chair. "Fine."

I struggle to catch my breath. "The other day, it seemed like this place helped to bring back some memories. Today, it's done the opposite. Am I wrong?"

Her eyes narrow.

"Does coming here help? Do you want to come back again?"

My mother nods. "Yes."

"Okay. In that case, I need you to show me. I'm about ready to tell that nurse you aren't well enough to visit again."

Her mouth gapes slightly, and she shakes her head.

"Let's try a do-over with another room. Sound like a plan?"

She nods, her expression still tense. Her fists are balled, and her knuckles white.

"Maybe this is too much stress on you. I was wrong about bringing you here."

"No! I want to be here."

I study her.

She relaxes her hands and drops her glare. "I want my memories back."

"What *do* you remember?"

Mom looks at the photo still in my hand.

I hold it up. "You remember marrying Dad?"

"I remember the picture."

"What about him?"

She nods.

"Does that mean you remember him?"

"Yes."

"What was his name?"

"Bill. That's what I called him."

She's right. Everybody else called him William, but at home

she did call him by the nickname. "Okay. Let's look around the rest of the lower level. Perhaps next time we can venture upstairs."

Mom twists her bracelet. "Can I have that photograph?"

"Sure." I hand it to her.

She takes it gingerly and looks at it with a wistful expression.

"Would you like to look around some more?"

Without a word, she steps over the glass and walks around the other side of the desk toward the door.

I catch up with her and stay next to her, but give her plenty of space.

In the hallway, Ember looks back and forth between us. "I'm going to clean the glass."

"You can come with us," Mom says.

Ember shakes her head and hurries into the office.

I turn to Mom. "You scared your granddaughter."

She frowns. "I know."

We wander down the hallway and peek into the library, the dance hall, and the other rooms. Mom stops near the back door and peers into a mirror that runs from the ceiling to the floor and has an ornate gold frame around it. Is she searching her reflection for memories of her past? Or perhaps seeing herself as the young bride in the picture she's still clinging to?

I start to say something, but then she turns to me. "I'm ready to go home now."

"To your room at the retirement facility?"

"Yes."

"Okay. Let's find Ember."

She doesn't budge. "You'll bring me back again?"

"If you promise to behave." It's kind of weird telling my mom to be good.

"I promise."

It's even weirder having her go along with it.

8

Ember

The shards of glass in the dustpan I'm holding sparkle in the beam from the flashlight of my aunt's phone.

Kenzi stands and turns it off. "I think that's the last of the glass."

"Finally." I also rise then dump the pieces of broken picture frame into the trash. "I never knew it was so hard to find all the tiny pieces."

She dusts off her knees and glances over at the desk. "What do you think she was looking for?"

I shrug. "Something to help her remember anything."

"It seemed like she was after something in particular, which was weird because she almost never came in here when Dad was alive."

"Maybe there's something in here about Jack."

My aunt holds my gaze for a moment. "Are you saying you think she knows more than she's letting on?"

"Or that she knows on some level. Maybe."

Kenzi lifts a brow. "And what was with her looking at that mirror by the back door?"

"That was a little strange." I don't admit how odd it actually felt. When Grandma was looking at the mirror, a cold chill ran through me—just like the one now. It's hard to explain. I mean, she was just looking at her reflection in a mirror, but it felt like so much more.

Like she could see something we couldn't.

"Want to watch a movie?" Kenzi asks.

I chew on my lower lip and ignore the chills running down my back. "I want to check out that mirror."

My aunt tilts her head. "You do?"

"Don't you?"

"It's just a mirror."

I frown. "I don't think so. Not between her talking about Jack and going through Grandpa's things. I'm not saying she's faking her dementia, but at some level something is going on. I want to know what—especially since it has to do with our house."

She doesn't look so sure. Or maybe she doesn't want to believe what I'm saying is true.

"We need to get to the bottom of this. The detective wouldn't have told you about your brother if it wasn't important, and what are the chances that Grandma is talking about another Jack?"

Kenzi hesitates, but then nods. "Let's go have a look at the mirror, but then we'll just chill. I'm ready to relax."

"Sounds good to me."

My aunt turns off the light before we head down the hallway, passing so many large rooms before we reach the tall mirror. It's the same as it has always been. Floor to ceiling with an ornate frame. It fits in perfectly with everything else in the house.

I scan every inch of the glass, looking for anything that

stands out. There isn't even a scratch. Then I study the frame, taking in every curve of the design.

A cold air breezes by, ruffling my hair.

I turn around, expecting to see that Kenzi has opened the door. But she's standing exactly where she has been. The door is still closed.

"What was that?" I ask.

"What?" She looks around.

"You didn't feel it?"

"Feel *what*?"

Tiny hairs stick up on my back. "Never mind."

I turn my attention back to the frame.

"I'm going to make some popcorn."

"No!" I whip around and send her a pleading look. But then I realize how stupid it sounds not to want to be left alone. "I mean, I'm almost done here. It'll just take another minute."

She lifts a brow. "Okay."

"Thanks."

I turn back to the frame and continue to study the wavy designs. The same pattern continues all around it.

"I'm going to the kitchen," Kenzi says.

Then I see it. A small square piece that doesn't match the rest of the design. It fits, but doesn't follow the pattern. And the difference is almost imperceptible. I never saw it in all my times here.

"You coming?" asks my aunt.

"Have you ever noticed this?" I point to the little piece.

She leans closer. "What about it?"

"The frame is enormous, and the pattern is never broken. Except here."

"Maybe a piece fell off and someone glued it back." She shrugs. "It's been here a long time."

"But it's cut perfectly. It isn't broken."

"It could be an imperfection to show its authenticity. You know, like how fancy paintings are numbered."

"Why would they do that? They could put a number on the back. But they didn't. It doesn't make sense!" Sometimes my aunt's refusal to admit this place has anything out of the ordinary drives me crazy.

She puts her hand on my arm. "I think what we both need is to unwind. If you were older, I'd suggest a glass of wine, but that's out. So, I'm going to make flavored popcorn and see if we have any ice cream left."

"Wait just a minute." I turn back to the frame and run a fingertip lightly against the unusual part of the frame. It's a little bumpy compared to the rest of the smooth wood around it.

"See?" Kenzi says. "It's nothing. Let's figure out what to watch."

I'm about to argue again when I accidentally push on the flaw in the frame.

It sinks in.

My heart thunders. What did I just do?

Creak!

The mirror slowly moves toward me. It's opening like a door.

It *is* a door.

I leap out of the way before it runs into me.

Kenzi and I stare at each other, wide-eyed. My face has to be as pale as hers.

She stumbles over her words. "What just happened?"

"That square you thought was nothing—it's something. A button!"

Without a word, she steps past me and studies the doorway. It's a dark entrance to ... what?

A musty odor comes from the opening. The air is warm and stuffy, the only sounds are of water dripping.

"What is that?"

She turns to me. "I have no idea."

My mouth dries. "We have to see."

"Not a chance." My aunt steps between me and the darkened doorway.

"What do you mean?" I exclaim. "We just found a secret room!"

She looks back and forth between me and the smelly doorway. "We *don't know* what we just found. It could be anything. Could be dangerous."

A thought makes my stomach tingle. "What if that's where the science experiments were conducted on people?"

Kenzi looks at me like I've lost my mind.

"There are rumors. And they must have some basis in reality! Look at what we just found!"

She shakes her head. "This doesn't prove anything. I'm closing this door—mirror—whatever it is, and I don't want you opening it again. Not until I figure out what's in there."

"How are you going to figure it out without going in?"

"I'm going to find the blueprints."

"You think something like *this* will be in those?" I exclaim. "Shine your light inside. Then we'll know what it is!"

She shakes her head.

"Then I will." I turn on my flashlight app as I push past her, and I shine the light into the darkness.

Stairs. Wooden. Narrow. Steep. They go down. To where, I can't see. My phone only illuminates a few steps.

My aunt forces herself in front of me. "We are *not* going down there! One wrong move, and that wood could give out. We could tumble down to our deaths!"

I can't argue with that logic, as much as I hate to agree. "What are we going to do, then?"

"Like I said, I'm going to find the blueprints to this place."

"You think that'll tell us if the stairs are safe?"

"It'll at least tell us *what's* down there."

I sneeze from the stench.

Kenzi closes the door. Mirror. Mirror-door? Door-mirror?

My mind races faster than I can keep up. How is it nobody knew about that? Which generation of Brannons kept it from the next? Did my grandpa know about it? His parents?

And how did nobody ever suspect it was there? It's an actual secret room!

Kenzi opens the back door and steps outside.

I join her and take in a deep breath of fresh air.

She's staring at the side of the house. "All that ivy has been hiding the fact that the wall here sticks out more than the rest of the house. I always just thought it was left there as decoration."

I take a few steps into the yard and take in the immensity of the house.

What else is this old building hiding?

9

Ember

K enzi and I are eating popcorn, but neither of us is paying a bit of attention to the movie.

"Where are you going to find the blueprints?" I ask her.

"I don't know anything about where those are kept. Maybe City Hall? Don't they keep records like that?"

I shrug. "You're asking the wrong person. I'm sure my mom would've known."

She nods, frowning. "But with a place this old, I have to wonder how accurate they would be—if they're even on file officially. There wasn't even a town when the house was built. For all we know, there were no original blueprints."

"Or they could be hidden inside the house somewhere."

"Maybe." She takes a deep breath. "And there's still the matter of finding out about Jack. If I have a fifty-year-old brother walking around somewhere, he might know some of this."

"He'd be that old?" I ask.

She nods. "Ten years older than your mom."

"Wow. If he's alive, he could have kids, even grandkids. That's so weird. What if I have cousins?"

My aunt frowns. "If he's alive."

"You don't think so?"

"Would I have been looking in the family cemetery if I thought he was alive?"

I shake my head no.

"Your mom never mentioned him, right?"

"Nope. Not once."

"That leads to another question."

I stare at Kenzi, waiting.

It takes her a few moments to realize I don't know what she's talking about. "Which Jack did that locked room really belong to?"

My stomach knots. "You think it was your brother's, not your uncle's?"

"It makes sense."

I suddenly feel like puking. "And that's the room where people say the light comes on when nobody's home."

"What?"

"I told you, this place has a lot of rumors."

"You never told me about that one."

"I also never said anything about the science experiments done on people."

She closes her eyes for a moment before opening them. "Our family is way more messed up than I imagined—even if only some of what we suspect is true."

I mull over everything I know about the house and our family history. My mind lands back on the old murder scene I found on the third floor, where the servants used to live. The police took the evidence, going as far as cutting into the ancient mattress to get all the blood possible to run DNA.

I turn to my aunt. "How did you say the detective figured out you have a brother?"

"I'm not sure I did."

"You didn't. How did he figure it out?"

She twists a strand of hair around her finger until the skin whitens. Her expression is conflicted.

"What is it?" I demand. "I'm not some kid you have to hide the truth from. You should know that."

Kenzi grimaces. "You're right, but you're not going to like it."

"There's a lot about my life I don't like—starting with the fact that my mom was killed. I think if I can handle that, I can pretty much deal with anything else thrown at me."

"You're right, but I can't say this is much better."

"Now you have to tell me!" I clench my fists, my curiosity burning.

She takes another deep breath. "Your grandma's prints were all over the knife."

"You already told me about that."

"I did?" Kenzi rubs her temples. "I guess I did. We need to figure out what it means."

"It doesn't mean she killed anyone." I try to imagine my grandma—who used to spend hours playing with me and teaching me about her garden—hurting anyone. It just isn't possible. "Like you said, somebody wearing gloves could've taken it upstairs after she used it to make a meal. Or she could've found it up there. Maybe that's why she and Grandpa decided to lock up that part of the house."

She gives me a sympathetic glance. "I think we might need to consider the possibility that she could be a viable suspect."

I give her a double-take. "Are you serious?"

"She—"

"Wait! If they found out those were Grandma's prints, did they find out whose blood was on the blade? On the bed?"

Kenzi hesitates.

"Whose is it?"

"An unknown male relative of ours."

I'm seriously going to puke. I don't want to ask, but I have to. "Jack's?"

"Luckily not. It doesn't belong to a close relative of mine— no siblings or parents."

"The other Jack?"

She shakes her head. "He died before Mom would've met him."

"Which brings us back to her finding the knife and touching it after the fact! Nobody currently living knows how Grandpa's brother died."

"It's a possibility."

"You don't think it's likely though. Do you?"

My aunt holds my gaze a moment. "I don't know what to think."

The room suddenly goes quiet as the movie ends.

We sit in silence, and I try to make sense of the news. Grandma might have killed someone in this house. Maybe not, but maybe so.

I turn to Kenzi. "Why wouldn't she have wiped the knife to get rid of prints if she was guilty?"

"That's what makes me think she didn't do it. That, and I don't believe her to be a killer."

"Can the investigators tell how old the blood is?"

"I'm not sure. It wasn't something the detective mentioned, and I didn't think to ask. I was focused on the other information he gave me."

"We need to find out about your brother." I tap the armrest. "It's time we go through those boxes upstairs."

"Right now?" she exclaims.

"The answers have to be in there. Why else would they be locked up?"

Kenzi picks up her phone. "It's almost eleven. I don't want to go up there this late." She shivers. "Let's get to bed. We can decide what to do in the morning."

"But I have the art camp all day."

"Good. That'll give us even more time to think about it."

"Don't you work tomorrow night?"

She shakes her head. "No, I have a lunch date scheduled. We can have an early dinner, then decide what to do. I'll look into the blueprints while you're working at the camp."

"Do you promise? You aren't just saying that?"

"You have my word. Pinky promise." She holds up her pinky.

I roll my eyes. "I'm not doing a pinky promise."

"Come on." She shoves her hand toward me.

"You're a dork, you know that?"

"I've been called worse. Do it, or you can't hold me to it."

I feel like an idiot, but I link my smallest finger around hers. "Happy?"

"Yes. Tomorrow we'll either explore the mystery room or the third floor."

"What do you think is down there?"

She shrugs. "Maybe a creepy old science lab?"

I shudder at the thought. "Well, if there isn't one in the basement, that could be. Do you think our ancestors were actually capable of that? Experimenting on people?"

"I'm beginning to think anything is possible at this point."

I was hoping she wouldn't say that.

A giggle sounds.

Kenzi sits up straighter.

"Who was that?" I look around.

"You heard that?" Her eyes look like they could pop out of her head.

"Yeah. Nobody else is here."

"Maybe it was the TV. Sometimes this streaming service starts a new movie on its own."

I turn to the television. Just a screensaver advertising another show. "Nope."

"Probably the house settling. You know how it is."

"Seriously?" I narrow my eyes. "You're trying to tell me the house settling sounds like a little girl giggling? The creaks and groans, I could believe. Not this."

My aunt rises and pulls her hair into a ponytail. "I'm sure it's fine. Nothing to worry about."

"You still going to try and convince me this place isn't haunted? That it's just 'lonely.'" I make air quotes.

"I can't explain all the noises. This house has history, and some events do seem to linger in a place. Just because we don't understand it doesn't mean it isn't real."

"In other words, ghosts."

"Or negative energy, or something else scientists haven't discovered yet."

"Like ghosts." I fold my arms. "I was right about this place being a murder house."

"We know of one person who died upstairs. It might have even been an accidental death. It's not a murder house."

"You're trying to tell me somebody died a bloody death *accidentally* with a knife hidden underneath clothes stuffed in an armoire—on a floor of the house that's been locked up for decades?"

"All I'm saying is we don't know the details yet. We may never know without a body."

"Oh my gosh."

"What?" She steps closer to me.

"You're not trying to convince me this place isn't haunted. You're trying to convince yourself!"

"It *isn't* haunted! This isn't a murder house."

"That's what you *want* to believe! Maybe even what you feel like you have to tell yourself. You grew up here. You've probably been telling yourself this stuff your whole life!"

"It's just a building!" Her brows draw together. "That's all. It's old. People die. It happens! Back when this place was built, do you think there was a hospital to take the sick to? No. They took care of each other within the walls. It's part of the history. End of story." She storms out of the room.

I hit a nerve.

And she's definitely hiding something from me. Maybe from herself too.

10

Kenzi

I pull down my sun visor, press my lips together, and check over my makeup. Everything looks good for my lunch date. My date is the CEO of a local startup who is also recently divorced. His ex, who has already moved on, will be there, and my job is to make it look like my date has also moved on with his life.

Shouldn't be awkward at all.

The morning runs through my mind. Ember was irritated at me because of our disagreement last night. She skipped breakfast and hardly said a word to me when I drove her to camp.

Being the adult, I should do something to try and fix this but I don't know what. Aside from the fact that I'm completely new to this parenting thing, the last thing I want to talk about is Billa—the probable source of the giggling. But that's exactly what Ember wants to discuss.

What am I supposed to do? I don't want this to come between us, but I'm probably going to end up on some type of anti-anxiety medication if I have to go back to that time in my life.

I can feel a migraine trying to start just thinking about Billa. She was my "imaginary" friend from my childhood. Billa would come to the house and play with me. She wore weird clothes and never wanted me to tell anyone about her. I loved playing with her because she taught me all kinds of games I'd never heard of and told me wild stories unlike any my parents ever let me listen to or watch on TV. When they found out about her, it landed me in therapy. Not just a run-of-the-mill treatment. No, my parents sent me to an inpatient facility because I wouldn't admit she wasn't real. They sent me away without a single tear shed, even though I cried and begged them not to.

At least I have all day to figure this out. Hopefully my subconscious will be working on it while I'm acting like I'm a CEO's new love interest. I'm grateful for the distraction. There's nothing like pretending to be someone else to pull me away from my own problems. Sometimes after a fake date, I walk away with the clarity I need about my own life. Other times, I just leave grateful my problems aren't as bad as some other people's.

I glance down at the time then up at the tall building in front of me. My date is supposed to meet me in the lobby and bring me to the meeting-slash-lunch in five minutes. At least I'm getting a meal. I was so worked up over my argument with Ember I didn't eat breakfast. Not to mention how tired I was. The giggling continued through the night, interrupting my sleep. Or maybe it was part of my dreams.

That's what I keep telling myself. It's a large house, and nothing sounds the same as in the tiny studio apartment I lived in before. I'm merely adjusting to a completely different life in a whole different state.

Not that any of that explains away Ember hearing the giggling too.

I draw in a deep breath and close my eyes for a few moments. We're both stressed and dealing with a lot of changes. Her, the loss of her mother and home. Me, the death of my sister and suddenly becoming responsible for another human as well as a gigantic house.

That reminds me I need to call someone to mow our lawn, but I don't have time now. I need to get inside.

My stomach roars. I better eat well. I'm going to need the energy to get through today. Finding a way to work through the argument with Ember without dredging up my past is going to take some work. Adulting is hard.

But here I am. I'll find a way to get it all done and somehow raise a teenager who hopefully won't hate me. However, she may need someone to vent her frustrations on, and I'm the logical target.

The alarm on my phone sounds. Time to get inside and meet my date. Leave my problems at the door.

I double-check my makeup and hair before hurrying to the building. The lobby is bustling—some people are standing around talking while others are racing from one place to another. Someone nearly knocks me over as he runs toward the door.

Another guy helps me before I topple backwards. "Are you okay?"

I regain my balance and force a smile. "Never better."

"Good." He returns my smile. "You don't happen to be Mackenzie?"

My date. I take him in for a moment—tall, expensive clothes, and kind brown eyes that match his slicked back hair. Then I hold out my hand. "I am. Pleasure to meet you."

He shakes my hand with a firm grip. "Wyatt. The pleasure's all mine. You're caught up with the situation?"

I nod. "Your ex will be at the business lunch."

Wyatt nods. "Unfortunately, yes. I appreciate you taking the job. I'm not sure how awkward this will be. This is our first time being around each other socially since the divorce."

"I'll do my best to help things go as smoothly as possible."

He tilts his head. "You've been in similar situations?"

"Plenty of times. I've seen just about everything in my line of work. Especially when I was living in LA."

Wyatt laughs easily. "I'll bet. Shall we head up?"

"Sure. Anything in particular I should know?"

He looks deep in thought as we head for the elevator. "We'll say this is a new relationship, so that'll explain it looking like we hardly know each other."

"Sounds great. I'll follow your lead."

As soon as we step into the elevator, his phone rings. He apologizes then takes the call.

I check my silenced phone to give him a sense of privacy. I'm surprised to see a notification for a message from Dayton on one of my social media apps. I had been on a date with him when I found out about my sister's death. The only reason we connected on social media was because I accidentally left with a pricy necklace he'd wanted me to wear to show off to his family.

He's going to fly me down to California for Thanksgiving for another family meal. Hopefully that one will go better than the last one. I'd had to leave his twin brother's engagement party after hearing the news.

The elevator stops on the tenth floor, and Wyatt motions for me to step off. I do, then he holds up a finger and points to his phone before walking about fifteen feet away.

I look out the window and decide to check Dayton's message, half-expecting him to want the necklace back even though he's told me multiple times to keep it. I read his message in his smooth British accent:

Hi, Kenzi.

I hope everything is going well for you in your new home. My

family is having a dinner for a cousin flying into Seattle this week-
end. Any chance you can join me Saturday evening? You may have
other plans, and I wanted to ask you before contacting the agency.
Let me know, and we can discuss the details.

Dayton

I nearly laugh. It's hard to believe he wants another date with me after the way our last one went, but now he wants two. One this weekend up here, and then the one over the holiday.

Wyatt catches my attention and waves me over.

I send a quick confirmation with Dayton since he'll see that I read the message. I'd been planning on taking Saturday off, but the way things are going, Ember and I could probably use the space.

A response returns almost immediately.

Great! I'll contact them and will see you in a few days.

I'm looking forward to it!

Me too. Send more info soon.

I double-check that my phone is silenced, then I join Wyatt.

"Sorry about that," he says. "It was an emergency from my financier."

"Is everything okay?"

"My ex is pulling some antics. She's trying to get me to fight fire with fire." He draws in a deep breath. "I refuse to do that during a business meeting."

"Let's kill her with kindness." I loop my arm around his and give him my best grin. "And show her that you've moved on and aren't at all worried about what she's trying to pull. That's the best way to win at this game."

His shoulders relax. "Perfect plan. Thank you."

A platinum blonde in a dress far too revealing for a business lunch rounds a corner.

Must be the ex.

Her expression hardens when she sees us. She moves closer to the man-candy next to her and glares at Wyatt.

I snuggle closer to my date. "Isn't the luncheon this way, darling?"

"It sure is, sweetheart." He wraps his arm around me and plants a kiss on my cheek.

The blonde looks like she could blow steam out her ears.

It's definitely going to be an interesting hour and a half.

11

___

Ember

I wave to Gretchen as she gets into the car. Before she closes the door, her mom leans over her. "Do you need a ride, Em?"

"My aunt's running late. Work kept her."

"I can take you home. It's no trouble. My dry cleaner's in your neighborhood, and I've got to pick up my clothes, anyway."

"Sure." I climb into the backseat, glad to be able to avoid Kenzi a little longer. "Thanks."

"No problem, kiddo. How are you holding up?" Her eyes are filled with pity.

It's the same look so many adults give me. Everyone feels sorry for the girl whose mother died. Why can't they treat me normally? I'm still the same person I always was.

"Fine." I pull my gaze away and send my aunt a text, letting her know I'll meet her at home.

"Just fine?"

"Yep."

Gretchen throws me an apologetic glance. She gets it. So does Kenzi, which makes me appreciate her even though I'm still irritated with her. Why does she have to insist everything can be explained naturally? We both heard that little girl's giggling, but she acted like she didn't.

"Mind if I pick up the clothes first?" Mrs. Ross asks.

"No problem."

The music is the only sound as we get through the downtown congestion. As soon as her mom races out, Gretchen turns to me. "What's going on with you? Seriously."

"What do you mean?"

"What do I *mean*?"

"That's what I said." I glance down at my phone.

Kenzi sent a text saying she'll see me at home. I don't reply.

Gretchen readjusts herself so she's looking right at me. "You've been acting weird for a while now. I think I've been patient long enough. What aren't you telling me?"

"About what?"

She gives me an exaggerated eye roll. "If I knew, I wouldn't be asking you, now would I?"

"I'm just dealing with a lot. That's it. My mom, the house." My voice cracks, and that stupid lump in my throat returns. "It's a lot."

"I know that. But we're besties. Something else is going on. You can't deny it."

"Fine! But I don't want to talk about it."

Both of her brows raise. "I knew it."

"Of course you did."

"Why don't you want to tell me?"

I clear my throat. "Some things are better left alone."

"What's the harm in talking about it? Might help you feel better. Our talks always do. I'm pretty amazing like that."

I laugh despite the threatening tears. "It's one of those

things that will feel a thousand times more real if I say it out loud."

Her smile fades. "What could be worse than what you've already been through?"

I glance outside to make sure Mrs. Ross isn't about to come in. She's holding her dry cleaning but still talking with the lady behind the counter.

"Well?" Gretchen taps her finger on the middle console.

I take a deep breath and my voice wobbles as I speak. "I found a letter from my mom in her things."

"And?" My best friend leans forward.

I swallow. "She gave me some clues about who my real dad is."

Her mouth moves, but no sound comes out.

I've done the impossible—rendered her speechless. "It's not much, but I know his first name and also the name of someone who might know more."

"For real?" Gretchen grabs my hand. "You've always wanted to know who he is! What else have you found? Tell me everything!"

Tears sting my eyes, and I blink them away. "That's it. I found the note, but I haven't looked for him."

"Why not? I bet we can find the guy by the weekend if we put our heads together!"

My hands shake. I move them where she can't see them. "I'm not sure I want to."

"Are you crazy? You've always wanted to find him!"

"I think he lives across the country."

"So? There's a thing called the phone. You don't have to get on a plane to talk to him."

I look out the window and focus on a crow struggling to get something out of a garbage can. "What if he wants me to move there? I'd have to leave everything. You."

"Then tell him no."

I turn back to her. "I can't do that. The courts would make me leave. He's my birth dad. Blood is all that matters."

"Your aunt is also blood."

"But she isn't my parent."

Silence settles between us before Gretchen speaks. "Then I'll hunt him down and make him move here. Problem solved."

"You and I both know that'll never work."

"I can be intimidating when I want to be."

I take a deep breath. "I just don't know what I want to do."

"Did you tell your aunt?"

"I haven't even told *you* until now. What do you think?"

"Maybe she can help. She might've met the guy."

I shake my head no. "Kenzi would've only been nine or ten, and it was a one-night stand before he moved across the country for college. No way Mom took her to that party."

"Wait. Your dad was just going to college?"

"According to my mom's letter."

Gretchen counts on her fingers. "He's a lot younger—your mom's a cougar. I mean, was. Sorry."

"Don't apologize," I snap. "Sorry."

She laughs. "I get it. Everyone else looks at you like they're thinking, 'poor orphan girl.'"

I grit my teeth. "Exactly. And she wasn't a cougar. It was one party. Richard was older than her."

"Hopefully your bio-dad is a lot nicer."

I just nod. The last thing I want to do is get my hopes up.

"So, what's his name? You said it was in the letter."

The front door opens, and Mrs. Ross takes her seat, putting her clothes in the spot next to me. "We'd better get going. I spoke with Carol too long. I'm going to be late picking up your sister."

Gretchen gives me a look that tells me we're not done with our conversation.

Less than five minutes later, we pull into my grandparents'

driveway. I mean, mine. When will my new life ever feel normal?

I thank Mrs. Ross for the ride, get out of the car, then wave goodbye. My stomach knots as I approach the porch. Part of me wants to check out the rooms Kenzi and I have left alone. Now we have that mystery basement to add to the list.

It's hard to know where to even start. The third floor has all those boxes—those are bound to hold answers. I picture old diaries and logbooks, but that would probably be too simple. Why would our ancestors make it that easy for us? But maybe they did. Although, it wouldn't surprise me if the contents leave us with more questions than answers. That's the way everything has been going.

I wish I had the hope of finding out more about my dad in the house, but Mom's letter to me didn't indicate she knew anything more than what she'd written. She never expected to see him again, so they parted ways without knowing anything more about each other than first names and their age gap—if she even told him she was about to join a law firm. She might've let him think she was his age.

I unlock the front door and turn off the alarm. The house always feels so much bigger when Kenzi isn't home.

Slam!

I nearly jump out of my skin. Once my heart rate returns to normal, I realize some windows must have been left open. Although, that doesn't make sense. If they had been and doors had been slamming open and shut all day, it would've triggered the alarms. Or would it only go off if the outer doors open? I have no idea since I'd only been half paying attention when the lady came and set up the system.

My stomach growls, urging me toward the kitchen, but I'm more interested in the mirror. A chill runs down my back as I recall Grandma staring at the mirror. It was almost like she was trying to tell us about the secret door. Did she know about it?

Hardly seems possible when she doesn't even know who Jack is. Not that we do, either. Her son or her brother-in-law?

It's so weird to think I might have an uncle somewhere. I mean, obviously I have relatives on my dad's side I know nothing about, but I can't believe my grandparents would keep a son secret. It obviously has Kenzi rattled to find out she has—or had—a brother. A dude who could be a grandparent himself by now.

Or he could be buried in the family cemetery I never knew anything about.

Slam!

I nearly jump out of my skin. Time to close the upstairs windows before I do anything else. I readjust my backpack and march up the winding staircase. A warm breeze ruffles my hair as I near the second level.

After I toss my bag onto my bed, a floorboard creaks behind me.

I spin around, expecting to see Kenzi.

But I'm alone.

Maybe I imagined it.

Yeah, right. I'm alone in the haunted Brannon House and a creaking floorboard is in my *mind*. My aunt is clearly rubbing off on me.

I close my door, look all around, then change into comfortable clothes before walking around the second level to shut the open windows.

They're all closed.

12

Kenzi

I pull into the driveway and check my phone. It had rung several times on my way home, but the afternoon traffic had been heavy, so I hadn't been able to check my calls. Even if it had been total gridlock and I'd been at a dead stop, I'd have been out of luck. My purse had slid onto the floor on the passenger side, so I couldn't reach my phone.

Once I finally retrieve it, I check my missed calls. All of them were from the retirement home. My stomach knots, imagining the trouble Mom has been getting into.

She'd been quiet and well behaved before Ember and I visited her and told her about Claire's death. I'd thought it was the right thing to do, but perhaps it'd have been more prudent to leave the old woman alone. It wasn't like she and I had any special relationship. And learning her favorite daughter had met an untimely demise had to shake her up, even if on the surface she couldn't remember any of us.

I'm tempted to ignore the calls, but I need to deal with this before I go inside. Once in there, I need to make good with

Ember, even if that means opening old wounds. If I want her to feel comfortable sharing her life with me, I'm going to have to do the same. In fact, I have to be the first one to make a move.

The last thing I want to do is talk about Billa, especially since that could make my niece even more convinced our home is haunted. I don't know how to explain my childhood friend. She felt real to me at the time.

The conversation with the nurse at the retirement home is quick. My mom has been demanding to return home all day and lashing out at the nurses. I tell her I'll think about bringing Ember by to visit her, but can't promise anything more.

Not after she broke the picture frame in Dad's office. And especially not after we discovered the mirror she was staring at is actually a door.

Before I think about any of that, I need to make things right with my niece. And that's a discussion that could go south fast.

My heart hammers as I step out of the car. I'm not sure I'll feel much better once the conversation is over.

"Howdy, neighbor."

I turn.

It's the neighbor I met the other day. Mr. Perfect Teeth, the self-proclaimed history buff. What's his name?

"I'm Dustin," he answers my unvoiced question. "You're Kinsley?"

I feel like he's faking his forgetfulness, but I don't have time to deal with it. "Kenzi. It's nice to see you again, but I need to get going."

"Have you had a chance to learn more about your home's history?"

"Not yet." I step closer toward the house.

"I noticed one of the lights was on all night."

"Oh? I'll talk with my niece. You know how teenagers are— night owls."

"That same light would come on before you two moved in."

That gives me pause. "Say that again?"

"It came on when the house was abandoned. When no other lights were on."

"Must have been when the house was broken into. We're still getting rid of some of the graffiti."

He chews on his lip. "Perhaps."

"Thanks for your concern. It's always nice to have a neighborhood watch."

"Glad to help. Have a chance to look into the house's history yet?"

Why is he asking me again? I push aside my annoyance and keep my tone light. "No. Still settling in, and that's quite the project in this place."

"Indeed."

"You know who you should talk to?"

Dustin lifts a brow. "Who?"

"My mom. When she visits, she actually remembers some things."

He raises his other eyebrow.

"She has dementia."

"You don't look old enough to have a parent with that."

"I have a fifty-year-old brother." If he's still alive.

"Ah, I see. Are you—"

"Like I said, I need to get inside. We'll chat later. Maybe when my mom is here."

He nods. "Indeed. I'll keep an eye out."

I'm sure he will. "Perfect."

Then I hurry to the front door before he tries to keep me out here longer. Once inside, I check to make sure Ember set the alarm when she got home. Everything looks good.

The house is quiet.

My stomach knots again. I hate that we aren't getting along, but people who live together have conflicts. It's just life. We'll get over it. We're family.

"Ember?"

Silence.

I'm hungry, but I ignore the pangs and head upstairs. I just hope she didn't decide to go exploring again. Last time she did, she got stuck on the third floor. I'm *not* ready to find out what's in that room behind the mirror.

I stop at the top step. "Ember?"

"In here." Her voice comes from the direction of her room.

Relief runs through me. She's probably getting ready for another day of working with art campers.

I make my way to her room, but hear rustling in Claire's room next door.

Ember is going through her mom's desk.

"Everything okay?" I ask.

She glances over. "Just looking through Mom's things."

I step inside. "For anything in particular?"

"Not sure. There are so many secrets. Maybe she left a clue about something in here."

"It's possible." I sit on the bed. "Found anything yet?"

She clears her throat. "I just got started a few minutes ago."

"I'm sure it helps you feel closer to her."

Ember shrugs. "It's still a little weird going through her things."

"I get it. It's hard to believe she's really gone and not just on a trip or something."

She frowns then turns away quickly. "Yeah. Sometimes I pull out my phone to call her. But then I remember I can't."

I get up and hug her. "I'm really sorry. If I could, I'd go back in time and stop the whole thing."

She nods, and though she doesn't return the embrace, she doesn't try to pull away either.

"I was thinking of stopping by the retirement home. Want to come with me?"

"You aren't bringing Grandma here again, are you?"

"Not today, no. I spoke with one of her nurses earlier and it sounds like she could, uh, use some company."

Ember pulls away. "In other words, she's been acting up."

"Basically."

"And you think we can help with that?"

"Maybe. I'm not sure what she's thinking. She could be worried we're upset with her and will never come back. If we go talk to her for a few minutes, maybe she'll make life a little easier on the nurses."

"I guess." She sighs.

"You guess what?"

Ember closes the desk drawer. "I'll go with you."

"You don't have to if you don't want to."

She shakes her head. "It's not that. I just hate seeing her the way she is, you know? Not remembering, but kind of remembering some things."

"I feel the same way."

Except I can't help but wonder if my mother knows more than she's been letting on. Between her talking about Jack and the fingerprints on the knife, it almost seems too convenient. What if Claire had been getting close to the truth, and then Mom decided to pretend she had memory loss, figuring a home would be less of a prison than jail? She could have even been working to get rid of my sister. It isn't a stretch *if* she already killed one person. Maybe more, considering my brother is missing.

Or maybe this house, its history, and the nosy neighbor are getting to me. That's more likely to be true. And besides, with the theories running through my head, that means my mom is —or was—potentially capable of murdering her relatives.

Two of her children down, one to go. Plus a grandchild.

"Are you okay?" Ember's voice brings me back to Claire's room.

I take in a deep breath. "Yeah. What were we talking about?"

She tilts her head. "Seeing Grandma."

"Right." My heart is hammering. I don't know what worries me more—that I'm actually considering my mother to be a murderer or that this house is getting to me. "Let's pop in on her. We can grab some dinner on the way home."

"Sure." Ember's looking at me like I could fall apart any moment.

"Let me just freshen up real quick, then we'll get going. We can talk about last night if you want."

She just nods.

I hurry to my bathroom and splash cold water on my face.

It's going to take a lot more than that to get me thinking straight about everything.

I just hope this house doesn't land me back in the nuthouse.

13

Kenzi

Our car ride to the retirement home is quiet. My mind keeps coming up with more and more twisted theories as to what happened in the house—and given how old it is, there are a lot of options. It's hard to know where to focus. Do I start with my mysterious brother? Or his namesake, our uncle who died young? The locked bedroom that could belong to either one of the Jacks? And whose blood was on that knife?

Everything leads back to my mom. The woman we're about to see who can't remember anything. Unless she actually remembers everything. The lady who raised me had a sharp mind. I could hardly get away with anything. I'd learned to be sneaky out of necessity since she and Dad were always so strict with me, never letting me live down my time in that facility.

It's kind of fitting that now my mom is living in a facility of her own. No, they don't force pills down her throat and tie her to the bed and—

"Kenzi!"

I turn to my niece, beads of sweat breaking out along my hairline.

"Light's green."

A horn blares behind me.

"Are you okay?" Concern fills her eyes.

I hit the gas. "Just got lost in thought for a moment. Sorry. Won't let that happen again."

"Does it have anything to do with last night?"

"I'm sorry I snapped at you. It didn't have anything to do with you. The house—it just brings back memories. Not all of them are good."

"I get that." Her voice is small.

Guilt stings. "I know you do. But I don't want to act like that. It's just ..." I let my voice trail off as I consider my wording. "When a memory strikes, it's like I'm right back when it happened. Some of the things I remember happened when I was really young. And I react like I would have then. I guess what's happening is I'm now forced to face ghosts of my past. Ones I ran from as soon as I could."

"Can you use any other word besides ghosts?"

I take a deep breath. "I don't mean literal ones. But yeah, I can probably come up with something else."

"Looks like we both have things to work through."

"Unfortunately." My breath hitches as the retirement home comes into view. "And here we come to one of them right now."

"You didn't get along with Grandma and Grandpa, did you?"

My chest tightens. "No."

"I'm sorry."

"Thanks, but don't feel bad for me. I should be the one helping you. I'm the adult here."

"We can help each other. Our wounds are totally different from each other's, so we can be strong for each other's weaknesses."

I turn into the parking lot, take the first available spot, and cut the engine. "You're wise beyond your years."

She glances out the window and shrugs.

"No, really you are. And you're right. We might be perfect for helping each other get through this. Maybe I can actually face my past and properly move on rather than fleeing."

"And hopefully I can deal with my mom's death before I end up running from it."

I lean over and give her a hug. "It's a deal. We'll help each other, and we'll be honest. I won't try to shield you from the truth or hide my past. But if it gets too much for you, tell me. Okay?"

"Good luck trying to shock me."

Silence settles between us for a moment.

"Should we go in?" I ask.

"May as well. I really hate seeing her like that, though. It sucks."

"What do you think the chances are that she's faking?" I blurt out.

Ember's lips waver. "I don't know. That's one of those things I really don't want to think about. I don't know what would be worse—her memories actually being gone or her doing this on purpose."

"Being deceived is far worse." I get out of the car and slam the door shut. If my mom really is faking dementia, our family is even more messed up than I ever imagined was possible.

I remote-lock the doors, and we head inside and give half-hearted greetings to everyone we pass.

Mom's room is a mess, but she's sitting calmly on her couch watching an episode of *Laverne & Shirley*. I recognize it because she had all those old shows on DVD when I was growing up.

Ember and I exchange a concerned glance as we step over items strewn across the floor.

I clear my throat loudly as we approach the couch.

Mom glances over at me. "Oh, Jacquie. So nice to see you."

"I'm Mackenzie, Mom. Your daughter." I purposefully use the name she always called me, despite the fact I go by Kenzi and everyone else called me that since I was young. My nickname had been my sister's idea, and I'd loved it from the moment it escaped her lips.

"Sit down." She pats the cushion next to her and turns her attention back to the screen.

Neither of us budges.

"What happened in here?" I ask.

"Laverne irritated Shirley by telling—"

"Not the show, Mom! In *here*. Real life. What did you do to your room?"

She turns back to me. "I don't know what you mean."

"Yes, you do. This mess." I pan my palms around the room. "Tell me you weren't throwing things at your nurse."

Mom blinks a few times but says nothing.

"You do realize they're here to help you, right? If you treat them well, they'll return the favor. I can't make any promises if you act like a toddler."

Her mouth falls open, and her brows move toward each other just slightly.

I've struck a nerve. She really is in there. How much of the dementia is real, I have no idea, but I intend to find out. And talking to her like I would have as a resentful teen seems to be pushing some buttons, so I keep on with it.

"Dad's money is paying for these people to take care of you. Don't make it hard on them."

Her nostrils flare, but instead of speaking, she turns back to the TV.

Ember gives me a confused look.

I nod for her to go with it, then I march over to my mother and stand between her and the screen. "Let's clean your room."

She scoots over and stares past me to the screen.

I move in her way again. "You made the mess, so you should have to clean it. But Ember and I are here, so we'll be nice and help you."

"I can't see."

"No?" I spin around and power off the device. "Let's get to work. We all know how much you hate living in a mess."

Her eyes narrow.

"Don't you remember lecturing me time and time again over the years about my messy room? Unacceptable—that was the word you used more than any other. I'm here to tell you *your* mess is unacceptable. Time to clean it up!"

The lines around her eyes deepen, and her mouth forms a straight line.

While I have her attention, I switch the subject. "Or we could talk about Jack. But the question is, which Jack do we want to discuss?"

Her lips turn white as her expression tightens.

"That's right, Mom. We know about the second Jack. Where is he? My brother? What did you do to him?"

My mother's mouth gapes, her face pales.

"Do you feel like cleaning yet?"

She leaps up, her legs far more nimble than I've seen since my arrival to town. "Nurse! Nurse!"

Ember throws me a pleading look.

"They aren't going to help us clean," I say over Mom's shouting. "You made the mess."

One of the nurses pops his head inside the room. "Is everything okay in here?"

Mom points to me. "Get rid of her!"

He steps inside the room and gives me a curious glance. "What's going on?"

"I told her we need to clean this mess. But she expects the staff to take care of it."

The nurse crosses his arms. "Really?"

"Take her away!" My mom shoves me toward him.

Ember gasps.

He races between us and looks my mom in the eye. "Regina, you need to keep your hands to yourself. Your daughter is trying to help you."

"She's not my daughter!"

"Yes, she is. Her name is Kenzi. She and your granddaughter are here because they care about you."

Mom narrows her eyes at me. "That brat has never cared about me one moment of her life!"

I put my hands on my hips. "So, you *do* remember?"

Her face reddens. "Get out of here, Mackenzie Lauder Brannon!"

We both jolt, and our gazes lock.

The woman with no memories recalls my full given name.

"Get out!" she shouts.

The nurse glances at me. "You'd better leave. She's been having a bad day. I wouldn't take it personally."

"We should at least pick up her mess." I look around him and glare at my mother.

"It's no problem. We'll take care of it."

"That's what she wants." I spin around and turn to Ember. "Let's get out of here."

14

Kenzi

After fastening Dayton's necklace behind my neck then adjusting it so the stones are centered, I check my reflection in the master bathroom mirror. I'm wearing a deep purple strapless, and the print on the dress has tiny pink and white flowers that are an exact match to color of the gems.

A giggle sounds from out in the hallway.

I ignore it, though my stomach knots a little. I'm not letting anything get in the way of tonight. I finally have the chance to return his necklace. Every time I look at it, guilt stings. It's way too expensive to be a gift, and besides, I almost never accept anything from a client—not that anyone else has ever offered anything close to this in value.

After pulling and tugging on the dress to make sure it falls just right, I slide on the same purple stilettos I wore to Claire's funeral. Thankfully, I was able to get all the mud off. Even I can't tell where the dirt was.

Then I touch up my makeup and add a little more hairspray.

Perfect.

I glance at the time. Ten minutes ahead of schedule.

Even more perfect.

In my room, I go through my shimmery black clutch to make sure I have everything I need for the evening. Makeup, check. Phone, check. Wallet, check. Keys, check. Don't need anything else.

Another giggle. Then another.

"Go away, Billa!"

Silence.

I don't know what's worse—the fact that I'm yelling at my imaginary childhood friend or the fact that she's following my request.

Dayton would never request me as his date again if he knew any of this.

I grab my purse and look around the room one more time to make sure I'm not forgetting anything.

Perfume. Can't forget that. I spray on my most expensive one and head out the door.

A rolled up set of papers catches my attention.

The original Brannon House blueprints.

It took me forever to find them. Going to the courthouse would have been too simple. I'd had to go on a runaround throughout town before finally landing the documents. While Ember was at camp the last few days, I was busy hunting these.

And they're incomplete. Neither the basement nor the secret room behind the mirror are there. And the top level is even less accurate, not showing any separated rooms at all. It does, however, show how much land my family originally had. Most of the town. It was sold off bit by bit over the years until we ended up with the section I currently own.

Ember and I spent a good portion of the night before making sense of the floor plans. I'm not sure which of us was more annoyed by what was left out.

That means the only way to find out is to explore areas that aren't public record. Rooms built that were never approved by any code. Not that any part of the house would've been built to today's standards. Or any other. Our house was built before there was even a town to have a building code.

I shove those thoughts aside. It would do me no good to think about any of this while out with Dayton. After ruining our last date, I owe him my full attention this time around.

A door slams down the hall.

"Ember?" I call, even though she's not home. She'd gone with Gretchen and a few other friends to a sweet sixteen party. After she left, I'd closed all the windows. Even so, I check them again.

The one in Mom's workout room is open.

A chill runs down my back, and it has nothing to do with the breeze.

I hurry over, close it, making sure to lock it, then I make my way down the stairs. It's a good thing I was ten minutes ahead of schedule before because I'm right on time now. And that's if I don't run into an unexpected traffic jam. I'm heading toward Seattle, so gridlock is a given no matter the day or time. I hope it won't be any worse than normal.

Thankfully, there are relatively few slowdowns on the way to the hotel. Dayton's family sure likes their gatherings in expensive places. It's no wonder he doesn't seem to care about me keeping the necklace. Doesn't matter. He's getting it back tonight.

As I park, I notice Dayton's imported convertible. I'm surprised he drove all the way up here when he could've easily flown.

By the time I'm done checking my makeup, he's tapping on my window.

I step outside.

"Hello." That accent gets me every time. He backs up, smiling, and nods toward the car. "I see you've upgraded."

I cringe, imagining what he must've thought of my old beater. "Money goes further up here."

It doesn't, really, but I find myself hesitant to admit I inherited it from my murdered sister.

He nods, then pulls out a bouquet of what has to be two dozen roses. "For you."

I just stare. Not that I should be surprised after the necklace.

"As a thanks for driving so far to meet me. You don't need to carry them inside."

"I, uh, thanks. It's no big deal."

He steps past me and places the flowers on the driver's seat. "They're in water, so they won't wilt."

"Okay."

"I hope you don't mind ..." He digs into a pocket and pulls out a jewelry box.

"What?" I exclaim. "I don't need more—"

Dayton whips the top off and shows me a delicate bracelet that matches the necklace.

"Really, this isn't necessary."

"My family will want to see that I've given you more gifts since they last saw us."

He reaches for my hand. In a matter of moments, he has the jewelry clasped. Then he glances back and forth between my wrist and neck. "Perfect. I love how your dress matches them. We're on the same wavelength." He points from my head to his and grins.

I force a smile but can't help thinking how our thoughts are so far apart they're actually on different planets. Different solar systems.

"Are you ready?" He holds out his hand again.

"Of course."

Dayton laces his fingers through mine and squeezes. His skin is soft, and his grip firm.

My heart rate speeds up. I don't know why I react to him like this. The last thing either of us wants is a relationship. He's a busy CEO, and I'm raising a teenager. Not to mention our height difference—it's ridiculous. Even with my highest heels, I don't reach his shoulders.

But those dark eyes and matching black hair along with that accent ...

No. I have more than enough to worry about. He lives in Cali, and I'm up in Washington. Not to mention things are progressing nicely with Graham. Nice and slow.

Neither Ember nor I are in a place for more change in our lives, and the last thing I want to do is throw in a wrench like that—with either one of these hot guys.

What is wrong with me? The house has to be getting to me. Memories of Billa and the facility my parents forced me into because of her. Daydreaming about a never-going-to-happen relationship with either of two gorgeous male specimens is my mind's way of escaping the past I can no longer run from.

That's the only explanation.

Dayton opens the door for me, and that's all it takes for me to push aside all my other thoughts. I'm on a job. It's time to get into character.

Once we find the banquet hall, I recognize a handful of people from the engagement party. Dayton's mom and aunt rush toward us from one direction, and his sister and grandma come at us from another. In a flurry of conversation, they ask how I'm doing after losing my sister and gush over the new bracelet.

I loop my arm around Dayton's waist after giving the women in his life hugs, and because they asked about my real life, I fall out of character and answer them honestly about where I'm living now—locally and not in LA.

My heart sinks and I throw Dayton a wide-eyed apologetic glance. What have I done? I'm supposed to be playing the love of his life.

He kisses my cheek and beams. "Yes, we're doing the long-distance relationship thing for a time while she settles her sister's accounts."

Relief rushes through me. I should've been able to think of something like that on the fly. What's wrong with me?

His mom beams. "Well, that's perfect."

"Why's that?" I ask.

She glances at Dayton before speaking to me. "Because Marcel has been trying to convince our Dayton to expand and start a branch of his business out here."

I have to think fast. I'm going to ruin this for Dayton. His business in LA is everything to him. "Oh, I'm *staying* up here. My sister has a lot of things to wrap up, and only I can do it. Then back to California for me."

"Marcel would be thrilled to work with Dayton," his aunt chimes in. "They haven't spent time together since they were boys."

I put both my hands on my date's arms and lean close. "Isn't that your brother over there? Let's go say hi."

We excuse ourselves and cross the banquet hall.

Then I turn to Dayton. "I'm so sorry. I fell out of character, and now I've messed everything up for you."

He takes my hand in his and gives me a reassuring smile. "Don't worry about it. They've already been bugging me about making the move—it's nothing new. I won't make any decisions that aren't good for my business. And I'm certainly not going to succumb to my family's pressure to do anything."

"Still, that was really unprofessional of me. I've never done that before."

"I don't blame you. They all know about your real life, about your sister's death." He gestures toward his brother who is talking with his fiancée. "Let's see how my twin is enjoying life as an engaged man."

I'm glad Dayton isn't upset with me, but I can't stop being irritated with myself. However, there's no time to mentally beat myself up. We greet his brother and his future wife, and I play the perfect part, not slipping up even once.

Hopefully I can keep it up throughout the meal and not give his family the fuel to pressure him all the more to make a business decision he doesn't want.

15

Ember

Someone shakes me, pulling me from a dream. I pull the covers over my head and ignore them. They continue with the shaking.

"Ember!" Gretchen says. "Wake up!"

"Go away."

"Your phone keeps ringing. It's your aunt."

"Then tell her I'm sleeping." I pull the pillow over my face, determined to get back to my dream and stay there for hours.

My best friend yanks the pillow from my hand. "It's noon. Isn't she supposed to pick you up now?"

I sit up. "It's already noon? It feels so early."

She grins devilishly. "Well, we *did* stay at the party until almost four."

"Then we made sundaes." I groan.

"And watched a movie." She sighs and fans herself. "I swear, Adam Dankworth gets hotter with every new movie."

"Where's my phone?"

Gretchen hands it to me.

Three missed calls, five texts, and two voice messages.

I moan. "I should've said no to the movie."

"Never say no to Adam Dankworth."

Still in a sleep fog, I call Kenzi back.

"There you are!" she answers. "I was about to worry."

"I was sleeping." I yawn, as if that proves it.

"So, I take it you aren't ready?"

"That depends. Are we just going home? If so, sure. But if we're going somewhere, then no. I'm not even close to being ready."

"I thought we could stop by the retirement home and see how your grandma is doing."

"Oh." I climb out of Gretchen's bed and look in the mirror. My hair is sticking out in every direction imaginable. I could pull it into a bun. I'll have to wash my face to get rid of the smeared makeup. "I guess I can get presentable enough for that. It's not like I'm going to run into someone I know from school."

"Great. I'll be there in five to ten minutes."

We say goodbye, then I hurry into the bathroom to make myself look as human as possible.

Gretchen joins me and washes her face in the sink next to me. "That party was so much fun. And I loved seeing you finally come out of your shell."

I turn to her, water dripping onto my shirt. "What do you mean?"

"You know."

"No. What do you mean?"

She gives me a knowing look. "You haven't been yourself since your mom died. I mean, I get it. Everything sucks for you. It's just fun to act like teenagers with my bestie again. That's all."

I frown.

"Hey, I don't mean anything bad by it. You know I'm here for you no matter what."

Ding-dong!

Kenzi's here. I finish washing my face and pull my hair back. No matter how hard I try, I can't even get a decent messy bun. I look like a wreck, and that's it.

"Don't be mad," Gretchen says.

"I'm not."

"You sure?"

"Yes." My tone comes out sharp. "I mean it. I'm just tired. Really tired."

"And you had fun last night. You can't deny that."

Images from the night before run through my mind. We danced with kids from school until midnight when the birthday party officially ended, then we went to another friend's house for an after party which was a little crazy. Gretchen and I didn't do anything illegal, but we had fun watching kids who did. They made total fools of themselves.

"See? Can't deny it." She gives me a smug grin.

"It was nice to forget everything for a few hours, but now I have to get back to life."

I can hear my aunt talking with Gretchen's mom downstairs.

"Is your grandma still being a psycho?"

"Don't call her that. But I have no idea. We've been giving her space to chill."

"Have you started looking for your dad yet?"

"Not so loud!" I glance toward the stairs to make sure Kenzi's still talking, and she is. They're discussing interior paint. I turn back to my friend. "I don't want my aunt to know I've been thinking about it."

"Why not?"

"I've already explained all of that to you—too many unknowns. This isn't the time."

She holds my gaze. "When *is* the right time?"

"I don't know, but it isn't now. And I'm done talking about it." I pass her, grab my things from her room, and go downstairs before she can push the subject any more.

Kenzi turns to me. "Ready?"

"Yep."

Gretchen comes downstairs and arches a brow at me. "Call me later."

"Sure."

Her mom turns to her. "You aren't dressed? We're going to be late for your sister's recital."

"And that would be the end of the world." She spins around and marches back upstairs.

My aunt and I say goodbye to Mrs. Ross before heading out into the bright sunshine.

"Did you have fun at the party?" Kenzi asks as she remote-unlocks the car.

"Yeah." I climb in and yawn, really wishing I'd said no to the movie. What had I been thinking?

"You sure you're up to seeing her?" She starts the engine.

"Why not? I'm just tired."

My aunt chuckles. "I remember those days. I'm glad you're getting back to your normal life."

Have I really been that boring lately that both my best friend and aunt are glad I'm going out to a party?

"Want to stop by a coffee stand?" Kenzi asks.

"Yes. That sounds like Heaven."

She laughs.

Ten minutes later, I'm sipping a salted caramel latte and starting to feel human again. Thank goodness for caffeine and copious amounts of sugar.

"Did you give that necklace back to the British dude last night?" I nurse my drink some more.

A beat of silence passes between us.

"Is that a no?" I ask.

"I might have gained a matching bracelet."

"What? You were so determined."

She stops at a light and shrugs. "I can't say no to that accent."

"Let me get this straight. He's tall, dark, handsome, rich, and has a sexy accent, and yet you aren't trying to date him for real?"

"Neither one of us is looking for a relationship."

"I guess why not, since you're getting paid to go on dates with him."

"Yes, he's a *client*."

"Bummer."

The rest of the ride is silent other than the music playing in the background. When we pull into the parking lot, I finish my super-sweet coffee then we go inside.

The receptionist stops what she's doing when we enter. "Nurse Nancy wants to talk to you before you see Regina."

Kenzi's face pales. "Is something the matter?"

"I'm not at liberty to say."

"Is Nurse Nancy available at the moment?"

The receptionist nods. "I'll let her know you're here. Feel free to have a seat in the waiting room. We just got new magazines."

"Awesome." My aunt's expression tightens.

I follow her to the waiting area and watch her pace. "I'm sure it's nothing."

"Nothing? It's never *nothing* with my mother."

"Can't argue with that."

I pick up a fashion magazine. It's over six months old. So much for the *new* magazines. But I flip through it, anyway. It's more interesting than watching Kenzi pace and mutter to herself.

Just as I'm getting into an article about mixing florals with stripes, one of the nurses enters the waiting room. She stands tall with a tight bun and an icy stare. "Mackenzie?"

Kenzi turns around. "Nurse Nancy?"

She nods. "Yes, I'm your mother's head nurse for the weekend. I'm glad you're here. I was actually just about to call you."

"This keeps getting better and better. What happened?"

"Would you like to talk in my office?" The nurse steps out of the waiting room.

"I'd rather you tell me what's going on."

"My office." She gestures for us to follow her.

"Then why ask if that's where I want to talk?"

"People generally just go with it."

My aunt mutters under her breath again.

We pass my grandma's room. I try to peek inside, but the door is only cracked open.

In the cramped office, my aunt and I sit across from the nurse at a small but tidy desk.

"What's going on?" Kenzi demands.

The woman clears her throat and plays with her collar.

Usually, the nurses don't get nervous. This can't be good.

"Just spill it. I know my mom can be difficult. Do I need to pay for damages to something?"

"Your mother escaped."

"What?" My aunt leaps up. "How did she get out? What are you doing to find her?"

My heart races.

"It's okay. She's in her room right now."

"What happened?" Kenzi demands.

"Have a seat, please."

"No! This place is supposed to be secure. A woman with dementia shouldn't be able to just walk out unnoticed!"

The nurse's brows draw together. "You're right. We have strict protocols in place and numerous security features. But somehow, she got out."

My aunt leans on the desk. "Tell me everything."

"Last night, one of our janitors found her outside. He recognized her as a patient and brought her in. Notified the head nurse on duty right away."

Kenzi's face reddens. "How did she get out?"

"We're still working on that. Somehow, she avoided the cameras, so we don't know."

"How is this possible?"

"I don't know, but I assure you we're looking into it."

"This is unacceptable!"

The nurse nods in agreement. "You're right, it is. We've fired one night staffer and have begun a full investigation. We are also tightening our already stringent security measures."

My aunt paces for a moment before turning back to the nurse. "Maybe we need to find a better facility—one that can actually take care of my mother!"

"That's an option, yes. But I'll advise you we are the highest rated in the area. Your sister picked us because there is none better."

Kenzi snorts. "Right. Well, thank you for telling me what happened."

"That's not all."

My stomach drops. Did Grandma get hurt on her little outing?

Nurse Nancy takes a deep breath. "I've had the head of security scrutinize our video footage. It appears last night wasn't Regina's first unsupervised outing."

"Are you kidding me?" Spittle flies from my aunt's mouth. I've never seen her so furious.

"No. She's come and gone several times in the last few weeks—that's as far back as our footage goes."

"Let me get this straight. You're telling me while under your watch, my mother has been sneaking out like a teenager, and this has possibly been going on for a long time?"

"We can't say how long."

"She's been sneaking in and out. That doesn't sound like typical senile behavior."

The nurse shakes her head. "No, it doesn't. An attempt to get out is typical. We stop those often. But successfully going in and out is not normal. I've already put in a request for her to be re-evaluated."

They go back and forth some more, but I tune them out and try to make sense of the situation. How on earth could my grandma be capable of that?

The only explanation is that she really has been faking her memory loss.

16

Kenzi

My mind is spinning out of control. I don't know who I'm more furious with—my mother or the facility. The staff should have caught on to her escape attempts long before they did. What was she thinking? More importantly, what was she doing?

This has been going on for who knows how long. A senile woman isn't capable of such a calculated thing. Not even close. Which makes me wonder—again—exactly how sick she was.

"Are we going to get out of the car?" Ember's voice brings me back to the present.

I stare at our house in front of us, unable to remember driving there and horrified at the fact. "I don't know what to make of the news."

"She has to have been faking her memory loss."

"But why?" I hold my niece's gaze. "What's the point? She could've been living here in the house all this time. Instead, she's been living at that facility for the last five years. It makes no sense."

"I have no idea. We should've tried talking to her before we left."

"Not while I'm this angry. I need to calm down and think about what to say first."

Ember's stomach rumbles loudly. "Let's eat, then we can figure out what to do."

"You haven't eaten today, have you?"

She shakes her head no. "I woke up right before you picked me up."

I have to take care of her first. My mother can wait, and she will.

We go inside, and I stick some frozen pizzas in the oven while Ember showers. It's all I'm capable of making at the moment. I pace the kitchen, feeling the walls closing in on me.

I really need to calm myself. If I don't, I won't be able to think clearly. And I need to make sense of the situation.

A child's laughter sounds from down the hallway.

"Not now, Billa!"

I'm losing it. I really am. Now I'm yelling at my imaginary friend. *Again.*

Thankfully, the shower sounds upstairs. My niece isn't witness to my insanity. I need to be careful before I find myself in a facility again.

And if my mother has her way, that's exactly what'll happen. Given that she has to be faking her dementia—who *does* that?—she'll be more than eager to get rid of me.

The woman is crazy. Certifiable. And that's her 'right' mind.

If I don't stop thinking about her, I'm going to lose it myself. I take a few deep breaths then check on the pizzas, which are almost done. We're going to need something to drink with that. I dig around in the fridge and find some root beers. They're in glass bottles, and I don't know where a bottle opener is. I ordered plastic bottles, but the store didn't have any, so they gave us these.

Everything is against me today.

I leave the pop on the table and rifle through some of the drawers, finding nothing. Bottle openers are the type of thing Dad would've had on hand. He'd have kept them in his office along with his stash of drinks. That was where he kept everything important to him, which is also the room I was hardly ever allowed inside.

Pulse drumming, I march down the hall to his office and fling open one drawer after another until I find what I'm looking for.

Then I stop cold. Goose bumps form on my arms.

Books lay on their side on a bookshelf.

They hadn't been that way before.

Maybe Ember was in here looking for something. Or she could've bumped them when she was in here putting everything back after my mom wrecked her havoc in here the other night.

My mother.

The woman who escaped from a secure memory care facility and who already had showed an interest in this room.

Tiny hairs on the back of my neck stand on end. Could she have come in here on one of her escapades?

No. That's ridiculous. Impossible, even. Between the distance and the security system on the house, there's no way. Not a chance. The system is so sensitive, Ember and I have both accidentally set it off. It has video and alerts us to every unusual movement.

I'm losing my mind. This house is actually making me crazy.

"Kenzi?" Ember's voice drifts down from the hallway.

"In the office," I call.

She comes in. "I took the pizzas out."

"Thanks. I didn't hear the timer."

My niece leans against the doorway. "You okay?"

Not even close, but I don't want her to know that. "Have you been in here?"

"That doesn't answer my question, but I'll play. No, I haven't been in this room since Grandma broke the picture frame. Why?"

I gesture toward the bookshelf.

She turns, then her hands fall to her side. "How did that happen? Those weren't like that before."

"Exactly, and that's what I want to know."

"You didn't knock those over?"

"Nope. And if you didn't, who did? Has anyone else been in the house since then?"

Ember finally looks at me. "I haven't had anyone over."

"And neither have I. You didn't see your grandma come in here after that, did you?"

"No. We purposefully kept her away from Grandpa's office."

"She had to have found a way in. That's the only thing that explains her escapades."

My niece looks at me like I've lost my mind. "Even if she's faking her memory loss, that doesn't explain how she could get here and get in unnoticed. She doesn't have a key. We changed the locks, remember? And besides, there's the security system. It's tricky."

"She watched me input the code each time she's been here."

"But she doesn't have a key. It has to be ghosts."

"There are no ghosts!"

Ember lifts a brow. "That's why you've been telling the giggling girl to shut up when you think I can't hear you?"

My face flames.

"See? Even you know this place is haunted."

"Your grandma has to have been getting in here somehow. Maybe she knows a way in that we never considered. An entrance that *didn't* get a new key—because we don't even know about it."

She folds her arms. "That makes less sense than a ghost."

"We both know the woman isn't senile. There's no way she could pull off multiple escapes if she were."

My niece and I stare each other down.

Ember straightens her back. "Where is this supposed secret entrance, then?"

Her eyes widen and her mouth drops open.

Realization hits me like a punch to the throat.

We speak at the same time. "The mirror."

17

Kenzi

M y hands shake as I stare at the mirror. Could my mother actually have been entering through there to get inside the house? Or am I truly losing my mind?

I don't even know which option I prefer. Which is scarier.

"Do you want me to push the button?" Ember asks.

"Maybe we should wait."

She turns to me. "Wait? Are you crazy?"

"I'm thinking about safety! Behind this mirror, or door, or whatever it is, is a room not on the blueprints. There are rumors of science experiments and murders. And do you remember the smell?"

Ember throws her hands in the air. "Fine! I'll go down there if you're so worried."

"No! If anyone's going down there, it's me."

"Then go." Her brows draw together.

This would be so much easier if I weren't in charge of her. "Okay, I will."

She looks at me expectantly and tugs on her ear.

I want to ask if something is wrong with her ear, but that would be procrastinating. I've noticed she plays with her ear sometimes when she's nervous.

Taking a deep breath, I turn my attention away from her, stare down the mirror for a moment, then push the button. I half-expect, or perhaps it's just desperate hope, nothing will happen. Maybe we're both remembering wrong and it never opened before.

Creak!

The mirror pulls open like a door. Because it *is* a door. It's been there my whole life, and I never once suspected it. Did my parents know the entire time? It sure fascinated my mother the other night.

I step closer, my heart thundering. The musty odor gets stronger. Something is still dripping.

It's so dark in there. The steps are so narrow and steep, they make the stairs to the third floor look like a luxurious walk in the park.

My skin crawls, my breath hitches. I'm primed to run the other way. But if I flee, then Ember will go down there on her own. The fact that she went up to the third floor alone proves as much. Besides, I'm no chicken.

Or maybe I am. I did move to California and never looked back.

But it doesn't matter. I'm here now. I've stepped up to the plate, and I'm raising my niece. I'm taking care of an enormous house, which now includes a secret room. Could there be others?

And I'm about to enter. What hidden secrets am I about to expose? Will what I learn be more traumatic than what I've already been through this summer? Could it be so awful that I won't let Ember come down?

I feel around for a light switch, and not surprisingly, I don't find one. Then I pull out my phone and shine the flashlight down the stairs. Can't see anything beyond the stairs. I'm not even sure I can see all of the steps.

After one step, I turn around. "Wait until I tell you to come down."

She shakes her head. "I'm coming with you."

"It might be dangerous."

"Then we'll face it together."

My mind races for a reason to keep her up here. "There might not be cell service down there. If I scream, I need you to call for help."

"I can come back up here and do that."

"You don't know that."

She folds her arms. "What do you expect to find? It's not like Grandma's hiding a dragon! How bad could it be?"

"Is that what you told yourself before going to the third floor?"

Her eyes narrow. "You're being ridiculous, I hope you know that."

"Better ridiculous than dead."

"Fine. I'll wait, but not very long. In fact, you have a minute."

"A minute?"

She glances at her phone. "Starting now. Better hurry."

Who's calling the shots? Me or her?

I spin around and step down. The board groans under my weight. I reach for the doorway and hold my breath, hoping it doesn't give out.

It doesn't.

My pulse drums in my ears, momentarily blocking out any other sound. I put my other foot on the stair. It holds me. I take another step. Then another, and another.

I'm surrounded by darkness. My phone's light doesn't illuminate much. The walls press on me. They're damp and narrow.

I place my foot on the next step, but it slips out from under me. I fall on my butt, scraping my back on the step behind the one I landed on. My grip loosens and I drop my phone. It bounces down the rest of the stairs, seemingly in slow motion, finally sliding, bouncing, and stopping out of my sight.

That could've gone better.

"Are you okay?" Ember calls down.

"Yeah, fine." I rise and dust myself off. "Just slid. Everything's damp."

"Gross. Can I see?"

"Wait." I press my fingertips on the walls on either side of me and take the most careful steps I can manage. My foot starts to slide again, but I catch myself before falling. I'm keeping my attention on the light down below.

I'm getting closer, closer.

Finally, I reach the bottom. The smell is even more pungent than before. It makes my nose sting, my eyes water.

But I don't see anything I expect. I'm not in a room. There's no secret laboratory. There's literally nothing.

It looks like a tunnel.

I have to let go of the wall to reach my phone. Then I shine the light everywhere. The darkness seems to overtake the brightness. It feels like it could swallow me whole.

"Kenzi?"

"Just a moment!" I take a few more steps away from the staircase and look around as best I can. The walls are made of packed dirt, and water drips down in places.

I go a few more feet. It doesn't show any signs of ending.

Could my mother have been using this tunnel to get in here when she sneaks out of the retirement home? I shine the light onto the ground. The dirt is so packed, I'm not even leaving footprints. If anyone else has been down here, they haven't left any either.

Has this place been abandoned for decades? Maybe it was used for Prohibition. Or something more sinister.

A shiver runs down my spine.

Something brushes against my arm.

My breath hitches. I freeze. Flash the light around.

Nothing.

"Hello?"

Silence.

I take a few more steps before stopping. Going farther would be stupid. What if the walls crumble? I'd be stuck, possibly without an air source. There's no telling how far the tunnel goes, where it leads. If it even has an exit.

Whispers sound down at the far end.

I'm done.

Drip, drip, drip.

Wheeling around, I nearly jump out of my skin. Definitely had enough.

I burst into a run, making it up the creaky, groaning steps in record time, struggling to breathe the whole way. At the top, I nearly crash into Ember.

She steps back, her face paling. "Did you actually see a ghost?"

I can't find my voice, so I shake my head no.

"What's down there?"

"It's a tunnel." I gasp for air, my mind spinning out of control.

"A tunnel?"

"Looks like it might go pretty far. It has to go at least beyond the main part of the backyard. I don't know where it ends. The woods? Farther?"

Ember steps toward the doorway. I'm ready to grab her and yank her back, but she doesn't go down. She turns back to me. "Why would there be a tunnel to our house?"

"I'm thinking Prohibition. But this place was already so far out of the way, I don't know why anyone would bother. I'd have to look into the town's history back then."

"If it's not that, then what was it used for?"

"I have no idea."

She plays with her ear. "Slaves? You know, that might explain the servants being treated so badly."

"This isn't the south."

"To keep them safe? To hide them?"

I rub my temples. "I have no idea. Let's close the door for now. We can try to figure it out later."

"Later? This isn't something we can just walk away from!"

"That's exactly what we need to do. We won't find answers now, and it sure isn't safe to check out."

"It's a *tunnel* that leads directly into our home! There's nothing keeping anyone from getting in that way. The alarm isn't hooked up to it, and I'll bet there's no lock." She stares me down. "We have to find out where it goes!"

"We need a plan before we go down there. And I do *not* want you exploring on your own. I hate to pull the adult card, but I have to. You could seriously get injured—killed, even! There's no way of knowing if the walls and ceiling are reinforced. They could collapse at any time. Do you hear me? This isn't a game."

She frowns. "Fine. What's the plan?"

I draw in a deep breath and hold it for a moment. "I'll talk to Gr—uh, Detective Felton—and see what he thinks." I don't want her to know I've been seeing him, even if the dates have been casual and technically for my work. The girl needs stability, and I'm giving it to her as much as I can.

"A cop?" she exclaims. "You think he's a mysterious tunnel expert?"

"Felton will know how to proceed. He looks into things for a living."

"You're really going to talk to him? This isn't going to be like the other rooms we haven't touched yet?"

"Of course I'm going to talk to him. This isn't just a locked room. It's a tunnel that goes to our house from who knows where."

"And how are we going to lock this door?" Ember looks around the edges. "There isn't anything I can see to keep anyone out."

Pressure builds behind my eyes and temples. "I don't know. Maybe the security company can come up with something."

"They'll come out on a weekend?"

"Probably not. I don't know."

She groans. "What about putting a chair in front of it? Or aiming a camera at it?"

"You think a chair will keep someone out?"

"One kept me in the third floor." She tilts her head.

"And that was a monster of a chair! We'll definitely never be able to lug that thing down the stairs."

Ember pushes the mirror closed. "That leads us back to, what's the plan?"

"I don't know. I really don't know."

18

Ember

My eyes close, and I drop my phone on my chest. I'm too tired to pick it up. Don't want to move. I've been trying to sleep for hours, playing stupid games to make myself tired.

Creak!

My eyes fly open and my heart races.

And there it is. Another noise to wake me, scare me, and keep me up longer. It's a good thing I didn't sign up to help at any camps this week. My to-do list has one item on it—get ready for school.

Okay, that's not the *only* thing. There are also a million things to think about around here, mainly why is there a tunnel leading to our house? I thought other stuff about this house was creepy enough, but that takes the cake.

A tunnel. That's the most absurd thing yet. I mean, really. If anything is going to be haunted, it would be that. Like Kenzi said, it's dangerous. But it couldn't have been any less dangerous back when it was being used. What if part of it collapsed and killed people then? That possibility has "ghost" written all over it.

I shudder at the thought. Not that it should bother me more than anything else around here. I already found an old murder scene on the third floor, and now my grandma, who may or may not be senile, could be responsible for it. And now we find out about her real firstborn, when we always thought that was my mom's position in the family.

Thud!

I pull the covers up to my neck and knock my phone onto the floor in the process. Tiny hairs on the back of my neck rise, making me feel like I'm being watched. I leave my phone where it is. It can stay there, I don't care.

Thud!

Maybe Kenzi is downstairs blocking off the mirror. I hate that it's an entrance to our house. The security system made me feel so much better. We're at the end of a quiet street with acres of woods behind us. Nobody would hear us if we screamed.

Just like when I nearly died in this house. A lump forms in my throat, and my eyes mist. I'd never been more scared than that night. I really thought that was going to be the end for me.

Creak!

I really, really hope that's my aunt. But it probably isn't. The house never really gets noisy until after she falls asleep. All the weirdness is probably normal for her. Although she was gone for a long time, so it seems like she would've gotten used to a regular, quiet house. Unless apartment living is noisier than this.

Seems hard to believe.

Thud!

Thanks for proving my point, ghosts.

I squeeze my eyes shut as tightly as I can.

Thud!

Clearly, closing my eyes does nothing to keep the noises

away. Maybe what I need to do is get up and face the sounds. They seem to be getting more frequent. I'm not imagining that. And it's not like all the ruckus has actually done anything damaging.

There are two options—at least as I see it. Either it's all like Kenzi says, just an old house settling, and us moving things around is making it more pronounced, or there are actually ghosts. Ever since we pulled up to the driveway with all my belongings, I've thought it looked haunted.

Nothing about living here has given me reason to think otherwise.

I'm actually kind of jealous of my aunt. She can at least pretend everything's normal. I'm not sure she fully believes it herself. Especially since I know she can hear the giggling because she tells it to stop.

I hold my breath and wait for the next sound. Probably a creak. Seems to be one creak for every two thuds tonight. Every night is different.

Bang!

I jump and tighten my hold on the blankets.

That was clearly the old ducts. But what never makes sense to me is that those aren't in use anymore. My grandparents switched all the heating and cooling to central air before I was born. When I was little, I thought those noises were the ducts expressing their anger about not being used any longer.

I'm not a little girl now. It's time to stop assigning meaning where there isn't any. I have to face my fears, and for now, that means proving to myself Kenzi's right—the sounds aren't malevolent. Or maybe they are, and I'm insane for trying to stand up to spirits.

Sometimes I wish I didn't have such an active imagination. I think I need to get back into drawing and painting. Then I can express my creativity that way instead of by picturing poltergeists.

My mouth dries as I push the blankets off. I'm shaking, but I ignore it.

I have to do this.

As I touch my bare feet to the cold wooden floor, I bump my phone. It skitters across the room. I freeze at the sound, and my heart hammers. After taking a few seconds to try—but fail—to calm down, I stand up. The floorboard protests as I put my full weight on it.

Creak!

My breath hitches. The sound is from outside in the hallway. I dash to my phone, yank it from the floor, clutch it to my chest.

Shadows move in the hallway, feet shuffling right outside my door.

I freeze mid-step. Can't breathe. Can't move.

Now the shadows go back and forth without making a sound.

I leap back into bed and pull the covers over my face. Tonight isn't my night for exploring.

19

Kenzi

Ember and Gretchen wave back to me as they head for the mall to shop for school supplies and clothes. I had offered to go with them, but they wanted to go alone. Not that I could blame them. When I was that age, I wanted to hang out with my friends without adults hovering.

I almost insisted because Ember has been so jumpy all morning. But it's probably just nerves from discovering the tunnel. We ended up carrying a table from the library and placing it in front of the mirror. It won't keep anyone out if they're desperate enough to get in, but it'll at least be a deterrent. And we'll be able to tell if anyone comes in. Or tries to.

When I checked this morning, it had been undisturbed. Not surprising since I got up at least half a dozen times to check on it and Ember. I kept hearing noises coming from her room. She must've been rearranging furniture. That's what it sounded like.

Once the girls are safely inside, I pull away from the curb and head for the coffee shop where I'm meeting Graham to discuss the tunnel. I'm not sure what I expect him to say. It's not like I think the police have a protocol for something like this, but he might have some ideas on how to proceed safely. What, I don't know. This can't be something they see often. But he has to have more resources than I do.

I hope. Because I'm way out of my comfort zone. It's one thing to explore a room, even one that isn't on the blueprints, but it's an altogether different matter to figure out where a mysterious tunnel goes. I've been trying to remember if I ever came across any sheds or doors in the ground out in the woods. As a child, I'd spent so many hours exploring and playing, it seems I'd have found something—if there was something to be found.

But then again, I might have found something and not have thought anything of it. With all the oddities in the house, a younger version of me wouldn't have given a second glance at a door in the dirt or a locked shed in the middle of nowhere.

Another problem with the tunnel is that the exit could have been destroyed decades earlier. My family had sold off property bit by bit, and if the tunnel had been purposefully kept secret, the owners at the time wouldn't have known they were selling something so important.

I pull into the parking lot of the coffee shop and immediately see Graham's bright yellow sports car. Is he off-duty? More importantly, does he think this is a date? A real one? I try to remember exactly what I said to him when I asked him to meet me. Did I say something that could've been misconstrued? I can't think of anything, but my big mouth tends to get me into trouble, so anything is possible. I'll just deal with whatever comes my way.

As soon as I step inside the building, Graham waves at me from a back corner and holds up two drinks.

It's definitely looking more like a date now.

I smile and wave back then make my way over. "Am I late? I

ran into some traffic by the mall. My niece is school-clothes shopping."

"No worries." He grins, showing a dimple, and slides one of the cups over to me. "I've got the week off, so I have nothing but time."

"You aren't going anywhere for your vacation?"

He shrugs. "Last week, my captain pointed out that I had unused time I'd lose if I didn't take it. Didn't really have time to plan anything. I don't mind a lazy week. But enough about me, how are things with you and Ember?"

I take a deep breath and then sip my latte. "Never a dull moment."

Graham lifts a brow and leans forward. "This sounds interesting. I'd have thought things would have calmed down since the funeral."

"My mother happened."

"Ah. Family drama. I've been there more times than I care to think about."

I set my cup down and spin it in circles. "I'm sure you haven't seen anything like mine."

He slides off his leather jacket and lets it fall on the back of the chair. "Try me. Most of my family is in the entertainment industry."

"*Your* family?"

Graham laughs. "I went a completely different route on purpose. Now I deal with a whole other type of drama. Traded in one for another."

"Now you have me curious." I sip my coffee. "Who's drama is worse? The old money or the entertainers? It could be a tie."

"Since you're the one dealing with it right now, why don't you start?" He puts his warm hand on top of mine, enveloping it.

My heart leaps into my throat. It takes me a moment to find my voice.

He looks at me with curiosity but not impatience while he sips his drink.

I manage to find my voice. "Well, the family drama is the least of my concerns at this point. Ember and I have discovered something in the house that makes me worry about our safety."

Graham sits up straighter, but his hand doesn't move from mine. "What is it?"

"We found a hidden entrance to the house."

He tilts his head. "If it's hidden, then what's the problem?"

"I'm pretty sure my mom knows about it, but that isn't all." I take a deep breath. "It's connected to an underground tunnel."

He doesn't respond right away. Just stares at me, unblinking for a moment. "You have an underground tunnel on your property?"

"Leading directly to an unlocked—and unlockable—secret door on my first floor."

Graham pulls his hand from mine and tugs on his ear. "That's intense."

Does everyone pull on their ears? I shove that thought aside. "Tell me about it. But that's not all."

He nods for me to continue.

"This is going to sound crazy."

"I assure you, between my line of work and my family, there isn't much that can surprise me."

I wring my hands together. "I think my mom might be using the tunnel to get in there."

And there it is. The look of disbelief. "She has dementia, right? And lives in the memory care facility across town?"

"I told you it sounds nuts, but hear me out. Her head nurse informed me she's been sneaking out. Do you know how hard it is to get in and out of there? I have to show ID every time someone new is at the front desk. The door is always locked and monitored. Someone has to let us in. A patient with memory problems couldn't get out."

His forehead wrinkles. "What exactly do you think is going on?"

"The only thing that makes any sense is that she's been faking her memory issues this whole time. What if that knife with her prints is proof of her guilt? Wouldn't it make sense that she'd cover it up?"

"That's really a stretch. That facility doesn't just let anyone in. The doctors are experts in dementia and Alzheimer's. And your mom has been there for a number of years, right? Long before your sister's death and Ember finding the knife."

"Yes, and I know how it sounds. It's insane, but we're not just talking a single escape. My mother got out multiple times! Nobody even knew about it until a janitor spotted her in the parking lot. And as far back as their videos go, there's proof of other breakouts. She could have been doing this all along."

Graham just frowns. "I can put your old murder case on a higher priority and look into it, but I can't guarantee anything."

I take a deep breath and hold it, trying to focus my thoughts. "Let's forget about my mother for a moment. There's a tunnel that leads directly to my house. Anyone who reaches the door can just walk in. I need to know where it leads, to find out how easy it would be for someone to go inside, travel underground, then walk into my house."

"And why can't you just put a lock on the door?"

"There's no knob. It's a floor-to-ceiling mirror."

He scratches his chin. "Your parents never said anything about it to you when you were growing up?"

I shake my head, not wanting to get into the fact that they never told me anything other than I didn't measure up as a Brannon.

"Is it possible they didn't even know about it? An underground tunnel sounds like something that'd have been built generations ago and eventually forgotten. Perhaps during the Prohibition era."

"That's exactly what I thought."

"From what I know about this area in that time, the police were on to a huge ring of bootleggers but never caught them. It had to have either been a really elaborate operation or someone on the force was paid off."

"None of that surprises me because my family could've pulled off either scenario."

His eyes light up. "I'd love to have a look around. Solve a bit of history."

I lean my elbows on the table and rub my temples. "I'm sure my house holds the answers to a lot of questions, but I don't want to turn it into a massive crime scene. It's my home, and I just want it to be my sanctuary. That's it."

"I understand. What *do* you want to do in regards to the tunnel? How can I help?"

I think about it for a moment. "Do you know how I can safely explore it?"

His eyes widen. "You want to go in it? The whole way? I thought you wanted to check your yard for the other end."

"I need to know where it leads, and I'm worried about it collapsing and trapping me."

"Have you already gone inside?"

"Only to the beginning. I thought it was a basement or some other type of room. I never imagined a tunnel!"

He nods, looking deep in thought. "Let me speak to some guys on the force. I'm certainly no expert in secret tunnels."

"Wait."

Graham lifts a brow.

"Nobody can prevent me from checking it out? You guys can't call it a zoning issue or something? Or forbid me from going in due to something else?"

"I'm not so much concerned about zoning as I am about safety. You're right to be worried about that—I hate the thought of you going in alone. Let me talk to a lieutenant who has experience with some mines. He'll know the best way to proceed."

"I appreciate it."

"And I'm glad you asked before exploring." He pulls out his phone and taps the screen.

"Are you texting him?"

"Just making some notes. I'll give him a call after we're done talking." He looks up. "What was the tunnel like from what you could see at the entrance?"

I sip my coffee before explaining what I saw, heard, and smelled down there.

He makes more notes as I'm speaking. "It does sound potentially dangerous. Part of it could've already collapsed. It's hard to say, especially since we know nothing of its history. Is there any way you can find out? Ask your mom? Look into records on the house?"

"I doubt I'll get anything out of my mom, but it's worth a try. As for records, there isn't anything on the blueprints. Not the official ones, anyway."

"What about the boxes on the top level? Have you looked in those yet?"

I shake my head no. "Ember and I have been more focused on making the living areas livable. I don't know when we'll get to the areas that've been locked."

"Given this new information, you may want to shift your priorities. The more we know about the tunnel, the more safely we can proceed with exploring it."

My heart pumps a little faster thinking about going back up to the third floor, especially to the room where my mother might have killed someone. That idea is looking more plausible by the moment.

"What do you think?" he asks.

I take a deep breath. "It's a big undertaking, but I'll do it.

Ember won't put up a fuss. She's been wanting to get back up there."

He holds my gaze. "I'd be happy to help, if you'd like. If not, I understand. It's family business. But it's also a massive job. Either way, I'd suggest you call a locksmith to make sure nobody *can* get in."

The thought sends a shiver down my spine.

Graham puts his hand back on mine and gives me a sympathetic smile. "Just let me know what I can do."

"I will. Thanks for taking me seriously. I wasn't sure how you'd respond. I know it's a crazy theory about my mom, but I just don't know what else she'd be doing when she sneaks out at night."

"They're going to make sure she doesn't do that anymore, right?"

I nod. "That's the plan. I hope they follow through."

"You think they won't?"

"It took them this long to catch onto what she's been doing." I finish off my latte.

He squeezes my hand.

My heart nearly leaps into my throat, and heat creeps into my cheeks. His effect on me drives me nuts. When I'm on the job, I have no problem taking the lead in these types of things. But those are also fake dates, fake feelings, fake everything.

This, however, is all new territory. Nothing fake about any of it. Especially not the way he keeps looking at me.

I usually keep people at a distance. Even my bestie back in LA. Misty would complain that I had an emotional wall to keep everyone out, including her.

She wasn't wrong. I've never liked to let anyone get close. And why would I? Growing up, the people who were supposed to take care of me criticized me and sent me away, disbelieving what I told them, accusing me of lies.

My job is actually perfect for someone like me. I get to

socialize and have fun without worrying about letting anyone in. In fact, I almost never see repeat clients because even that allows people to be too close.

Maybe I've always enjoyed the fakeness more than I've let myself believe.

Now I've got this kind-hearted gorgeous cop looking at me like he might want to take things to the next level.

I pull my hand away from his and look at the time. "I've got to pick up Ember. We'll talk after you've spoken with the lieutenant?"

"Sure." The disappointment in his expression is undeniable. "And you'll see if you can get anything out of your mom?"

"Today."

"Great. Let me know if you need an extra hand going through those boxes."

"Thanks, I appreciate it." I think my tone gives away that I don't intend to ask for his help.

More disappointment in his eyes.

Guilt stings. But it isn't nearly as noticeable as my urge to burst into a run and flee the coffee shop.

20

Kenzi

I squeeze the steering wheel as I stare at the memory care facility in front of me. I'd almost rather invite Graham over to unbox the third floor of my house than go inside and question my mother. But this needs to be done.

Ember wanted to stay at the mall with Gretchen and some other girls they'd run into. Who was I to say no to that? My niece has spent way too much time at home with me, working on the house. She needs girl time. With any luck, she won't end up as closed off as me, won't have problems connecting with people like I do.

Besides, this isn't going to be a fun conversation. I may as well do it on my own.

When I get inside, the girl at the counter who has seen me numerous times, takes my ID before letting me back to where the patients are. I'm glad to see they're upping their security measures.

Mom is in her room watching black and white reruns. No surprise there. She's probably going to double down on her dementia act now. I'll be lucky to get anything out of her. I'm still not sure if I'm going to bring up the tunnel or not. I am curious to see her reaction when hearing that I know about it.

"How are you doing, Mom?" I ask loudly.

If she hears me, she doesn't respond.

I step over to the couch and repeat my question. "How are you doing, Mom?"

She doesn't look away from the screen.

I sit uncomfortably close to her. "Whatcha watching?"

No response.

It's tempting to get frustrated, but I'm not going to give in to her. My plan is to act like this is just another job. She's a client, and I'm supposed to learn more about her. Easy peasy.

If only.

"Ember's shopping for clothes with her friends. Can you believe school will be starting soon?"

Mom doesn't reply.

"Do you remember when I was in school?" I lean back and take a deep breath. "I used to love shopping for a whole new wardrobe. You always said I'd bleed your bank account dry."

She laughs along with the canned laughter from the show, not indicating she's aware I'm next to her.

"At least I never bought that many clothes, or you wouldn't be able to stay here. Right?"

She jolts, just slightly. I might not have even noticed if I hadn't been looking for it.

"Do you like staying here? Is it nice having people do everything for you?" I wait for a response before continuing. "I hear you've been enjoying some field trips. Is that true?"

Mom doesn't even blink.

"Where have you been going? Anywhere interesting?"

Now she blinks, her lips pursing together tightly. She knows exactly what I'm talking about.

"Visiting the house? Are you the one behind the noises Ember and I have been hearing at night?"

Now she's blinking rapidly.

"Or maybe you've been visiting Jack's grave? Or calling him? Which is it, Mom? I'm dying to know."

She turns to me, her brows furrowed and her nostrils flaring.

"Why didn't you ever tell me about Jack? Did Claire know about him?"

Mom breathes heavily, her chest heaving.

"Why all the secrets? I'm going to find out one way or another. I wish you'd just tell me yourself. Make things right for once."

Her eyes narrow, and her lips turn white from pressing them together so hard.

"What's the point in all of this? Why pretend to have no memories? I don't get it. You'd take this over living in your own home? Why let it go to ruin? Why?"

"Shut up!"

"I'm not a child you can silence. And I'm definitely not going to stop looking into any of this. I want answers, and I'm going to get them one way or another. You can make it easy on me and answer my questions, or you can make it difficult. Either way, I'm going to get to the truth."

She stares at me, breathing hard.

I'm getting somewhere. I might not get much further today, but it's at least progress. I'll take it.

"Why won't you talk about Jack? Is he out there somewhere? Or buried in a secret plot?"

"Go away."

I shake my head no. "I'm not going to stop until I get answers. I have no reason to believe you aren't operating under your full senses. But here's the thing—you're here and I'm at home. You can't sneak in there. Can't go anywhere without me signing you out. Tell me what you're hiding, and I can help you. Don't you want to live a life of freedom? To come back home and work on your garden? To—" I freeze. "Wait a minute. Your *garden*. That's where he is, isn't he?"

"I don't know what you're talking about."

"But you *do* know we aren't living in an episode of *I Love Lucy*. What are we going to find if we excavate your garden?"

She squeezes her fists, scoots away from me.

"Whatever clues you've left behind at the house, I can find. It might take a while, but I'll get there. It's only a matter of time, and that's something I have plenty of."

"Go ahead and try." She turns back to the TV and hums a tune.

"What should I check first? Your garden or the tunnel?"

Mom turns to me, her eyes wide and her face pale. "What did you say?"

"You heard me."

"A tunnel?"

It's my turn to not blink, not reply.

"How do you know about that?"

I study her before answering. "You made it pretty obvious the way you were staring at the mirror which is actually a door. I'm going to have a locksmith put in a lock."

"You can't do that!"

"I can't?"

"No! That's a piece of history."

"History? That's what you're worried about?"

She plays with the hem of her shirt.

"Are you sure you aren't more concerned about not being able to sneak in? But it's your own house. Why not just live there if you want in so badly?"

"You wouldn't understand. Go away."

"Why wouldn't I understand?"

Mom turns back to the screen and changes the channel from a laundry commercial. "Leave."

"Ember and I are your only remaining relatives. Why not let us in? Tell us what's really going on."

She shakes her head.

"Is that no, you won't tell us? Or no, we aren't your only living family?"

No response.

"Okay, then. I'll make the phone call to have the tunnel checked out for safety. Then I'll tear the house apart to find out why it was built. Secrets are always uncovered, and I'm going to lay these bare."

My mother turns back to me. "You would turn our house into a spectacle? Open up everything for public display?"

"Why wouldn't I? I don't know anything about any of it. You and Dad have kept everything from me, not allowing me inside nearly half our house. Not telling me the history. I don't know any more than neighbors whispering rumors. You want the secrets to remain hidden? Then you'd better start talking."

"You're threatening me? Me?"

"No. I'm simply letting you know what's going to happen. I need answers about the house I'm living in, and I can either find them myself or you can tell me what you know."

"Some things are meant to stay buried."

"Like Jack?"

"You know nothing about him!"

"Precisely. You've kept my brother a secret from me my entire life. Why?"

"I'm done. For the final time, go away." My mother scoots even farther from me and focuses her attention on the show.

My blood seems to flow slower. It's harder to take a deep breath. My suspicions have been confirmed—some of them. Enough that I know I'm on the right track. She doesn't have dementia, and I do have a brother who would be or is fifty years old. Mom knows about the tunnel.

Now I have more questions, but I'm not going to get any answers today.

Or will I?

"One more thing, Mom."

She groans, but doesn't pull her attention away from the TV.

"Since you don't have any memory issues, I'm going to have to look into moving you to a different facility."

"What?" She whips toward me.

"This place is for people with memory issues."

"You can't prove anything!"

"Can't I?" I turn toward the door.

Dr. Tribble walks in. "Regina, you've made a miraculous recovery."

Mom stares at him, then back to me, her mouth gaping.

I rise and turn to the doctor. "Call me when you're done discussing this with her."

"Will do. Thank you, Ms. Brannon."

21

Ember

My heart hammers as Kenzi reaches for the door to the third floor. I can't believe we're actually going up there to explore the contents of the boxes. And even more, I can't believe I'm going up there again. The two other times I'd been in there hadn't gone well for me—I'd gotten locked in the first time and had my life threatened by two psychopaths the second time.

Neither of those events were going to happen now. My aunt and I are going up there together, and we know what we're facing. Boxes. That's it. I don't know about her, but I'm going to avoid the murder room. There are more than enough things to go through in the other areas of the third floor.

Kenzi looks at me, her hand on the knob. "You ready?"

"I hope so. Can we bring the boxes down here to open?"

"If they're light enough to carry down the stairs."

I frown. "Do you think they will be? The wooden boxes themselves look weighty."

She hands me a dust mask. "Between these and opening the windows, we'll be fine."

Neither will keep ghosts away, but I keep that thought to myself. My aunt only ever wants to focus on what can be seen. "What if the breeze makes the door slam shut?"

"It would have to travel all the way down the staircase. Highly unlikely. And besides, it doesn't lock anymore. Remember?" She twists the knob as if to prove the point.

"It wasn't the lock that got me into trouble before. Someone pushed that heavy chair in front of the door. And the other time I was dragged—"

"That's in the past. You're safe now. My mother isn't getting out of her facility. Nobody other than us has a key. We're good. Take my word for it."

Ghosts don't use keys, but again, I don't say anything. I look around for something to prop the door open and find a small chair. I drag it over to the door. It works perfectly.

"Do you feel better?" Kenzi asks.

"Much."

"Great. Let's do this." She puts on her mask and starts up the creaky stairs.

My pulse drums in my ears as I follow her. I take deep breaths, inhaling dust, and remember to put on my mask too. Everything is going to be fine. It's all like my aunt said. Nobody is going to try to kill us. Even if there are spirits, they aren't malevolent. They haven't tried to hurt us—not like some people.

Kenzi stops at the landing at the top of the narrow stairs. "Should we start with the first room?"

"It's as good as any." We kick up dust with our feet. It's worse than before now that so many people have been up here.

Everything in the room is still covered in at least an inch.

My aunt fights with the small window. I help her, and even with both of us straining, it won't budge.

I wipe dust on my pants. "Our ancestors probably didn't want them trying to escape."

"Or it's just stuck from so many years of not being used."

"Maybe both."

We try again, until sweat breaks out on my forehead. I must have put on the mask wrong because now I'm coughing and it feels like something is in my throat. But I keep pulling on the window, even though it won't do any good open.

I step back, still coughing. "Let's forget about the window."

She keeps yanking. "I ... think ... it's ... about ... to ... budge."

I'm half-tempted to get a picture of her in her super-stylish clothes and nearly perfect hair trying to open a window in what has to be the dustiest place in the entire town.

She stops, huffs and puffs, then wipes a streak of dust across her face and through her hair. "We might need someone to help us get that open."

"Who? Like that history-crazy neighbor?"

Her brows draw together. "You've met him?"

"He introduced himself earlier when Gretchen and her mom dropped me off."

"I don't trust him."

"You don't? He seemed nice."

"Don't trust anyone obsessed with the house. I don't know what his angle is, and I don't care to find out."

I move past her and yank on the window. My hand slips and I break a nail. "I'm done."

"Me too. It's not budging. If Dustin talks to you again, let me know."

"Why?"

"I just want to know. Was today the first time he spoke to you?"

"Yep. Haven't met many neighbors since we moved in. He might be the first, actually."

"We probably should reach out to them, but later. Should

we take separate boxes or go through them one by one together?"

I sneeze. "Doesn't matter to me."

She places a hand on the top of a wooden box on one pile. "I'll start with this one."

"Let me help you get it down. It looks heavy."

Together we get it to the floor, barely. It weighs even more than it looked like it would.

I take a deep breath. "Maybe we should work together instead."

Kenzi pulls her hair back into a messy bun, strands sticking to her neck. "Sounds like a plan."

I pull off the top and set it on the bed, creating a massive plume of dust. "I didn't think that through."

She laughs and coughs. "And I didn't get strong enough masks."

We lean over the box to find the contents covered in a yellowed sheet. I reach for it but then my eye starts to burn as some dust gets in, but I manage to get it out.

"Are you okay?" she asks.

"Something in my eye."

"Maybe we should come back with better masks and eye protection. And perhaps bring someone who can help us with the windows."

"I don't need anything for my eyes. It was only a fleck of dust—surprisingly enough."

Kenzi chuckles. "I'm just saying, it might be nice to have some help."

"Gretchen really wants to see what's up here."

"And the detective offered to help."

"The detective?" I arch a brow. "When did you see him?"

She shifts her weight and looks away. "Well, I asked him what he thought about the tunnel. I'm serious about taking every possible safety precaution."

"Do the police really need to be involved? And why are you acting weird?"

"Weird? What do you mean?"

"You looked away when I mentioned him."

"That's not acting strange. I'm just trying to figure out what to do. Being up here is a safety issue, as well. This dust isn't healthy. Maybe we should come back."

"Not a chance. It's taken us this long to get up here. I'm not turning back now."

She finally meets my gaze. "And neither am I. We need answers, and my mother isn't giving us anything, even though it's clear she hasn't forgotten a single thing."

"What's going to happen to her?"

"How do you mean?"

"If she really doesn't have dementia, she can't stay at that facility. Or can she?"

My aunt mumbles something I can't make out.

"What's that?"

"Let's just take this one thing at a time. The doctor said it'll take some time to figure out what's going on. That's the first step. Just like our first step is to get through this box. There's no way we're going to get it downstairs ourselves. Do you want to go through it or wait?"

"Is that even a question?" I grab the sheet and put it on the bed, ignoring the new cloud of dust.

She turns around, coughing.

Maybe we really do need different masks. Who knows what's in those particles? Old diseases we aren't immune to? Or would our ancestors have passed along the immunity to us?

Kenzi turns back around. "Ready to look?"

My breath hitches. "Let's do this."

Are we about to find answers?

We both look down. The box is filled with books.

She picks one up from the top. "No wonder it was so heavy."

"What's that book?" I pick up a different one and open it, careful with the fragile pages. This one is a logbook of some sort. It's filled with numbers in a light, curvy script.

"Receipts. Notes about purchases." She holds it up for me to see. "It's all pretty faded. What do you have?"

"Basically the same, but no receipts. Just handwriting."

"Any dates?"

I scan the page, not seeing any. Then I check the next few, still not seeing dates. Just a bunch of addition and subtraction problems. Not very interesting. Definitely no answers about any murder.

After going through each page, we set the books aside and pick up more from the box. I get another receipt book. "What do you have?"

Kenzi turns to me. "Photos."

I drop the logbook and scurry around the box to see the pictures. They're sepia, and the people are dressed like pictures I've seen from the Depression era.

The same time period as Prohibition, if I'm remembering my history lectures right. I never thought it was something I'd ever need. Could these people have made the tunnel? Or had it already been there? Did they even know about it?

My aunt flips through the pages like a sloth stuck in molasses.

"Are there any pictures of the *tunnel*?" I try to peek at pages further back.

"Look at these clothes. They're amazing."

Of course she's more concerned about fashion. "Yeah, great. What about the tunnel?"

She frowns. "You really think they would've taken pictures of it? Of something they wanted to keep secret?"

"Why not? Seems our relatives could get away with anything they wanted."

"Not likely. It wasn't easy to get photos back then. A photographer would have to come to the house, then the film would have to be developed. There were no smart phones back then. It was a whole different world."

"I know that." I throw her an exasperated look. "But maybe they did get pictures. They had to have been proud of it, especially if they built it. Why not get photo proof? They wouldn't display them around the house, but I think they'd want them."

"It's possible." She flips a page. "Look at these dresses! Women didn't wear these for special occasions. They dressed like this every day."

"Focus. We can gawk at the clothes any time. We're here to uncover family secrets."

She pulls the photo album closer. "Check this out. This lady looks a lot like your mom."

"Really?" I crane my neck and study the picture she's pointing to. The woman in the picture does look a lot like my mom did when she was younger. "That's so weird. Anyone look like me? Or you?"

"Now who's the one getting distracted?" Kenzi teases.

I take the book from her and gingerly flip to the next page. "This dude looks just like Grandpa, except constipated."

My aunt laughs. "Most people didn't smile in photos back then. They didn't have the dental care we do."

"This girl is smiling."

"Her mouth is still closed."

I scan the page for anyone truly smiling and don't find any. "I would've. Smiling makes people look so much better."

We flip through the pages, commenting on clothes and expressions. It's hard to believe we're related to all of them. Or at least most of them. Some might've been friends of the family. It's fun to see who resembles people we know.

Creak!

Kenzi and I both freeze and look around, wide-eyed.

Creak-creak.

My pulse races, my breathing hitches. I look around for a weapon. Memories of being forced up here flash through my mind. I need to start carrying a pocket knife at the very least.

After a full minute passes, my aunt finally speaks. "It's just the house settling."

Creak.

Color drains from her face.

"You sure about that?"

She doesn't answer.

A cold chill runs through me.

Slam!

Was that the door at the bottom of the stairs? The one I propped open with a chair?

My gaze locks on Kenzi's. Without a word, we both hurry out of the room and to the top of the stairs.

The door is closed.

22

Ember

My legs feel like rubber. They won't move. I can hardly breathe.

I put a chair in front of that door. Now it's closed. It couldn't have been a draft. We never got the window open upstairs. And even if we had, Kenzi's right—it would never cause the door to close. No breeze could make it down there, and even if one did, the door was propped open.

Yet now it's closed. Slammed shut. I can still hear the sound echoing in my head.

My aunt moves past me and creeps down the stairs, clinging to the railing which looks like it could fall off with one wrong move.

I can't let her go down by herself. There's either a person down there—someone who broke in—or a ghost with the power to move physical objects.

I'm not sure which prospect scares me more.

Somehow, I manage to get my feet to move. On the stairs, I cling to the railing just like Kenzi does. It'll probably collapse under our weight, but at the moment, I don't care. It's keeping me steady. Finally, I catch up with her.

She reaches for the knob.

I hold my breath in anticipation. It's going to be locked, I just know it. Even though it has a new knob without a locking mechanism. Or maybe it'll be covered in protoplasm and we won't be able to twist it.

It twists. She pushes the door open. Turns to me, brings her finger to her mouth, and motions for me to stay put.

Like that's going to happen.

Kenzi steps onto the hardwood floor and looks around, her hand still on the knob.

My heart feels like it's going to explode out of my chest. I can hardly breathe.

She inches out until she has to let go of the door.

I follow, careful to keep my steps light. She can't tell me to go back if she doesn't know I'm right behind her.

My aunt looks up and down the hall.

I follow her gaze, seeing nothing.

We're going to die, there's no other possible outcome. I'm going to join my mom before I even have the chance to finish high school.

Kenzi whips around and nearly crashes into me. Her eyes widen. Then she glares at me and motions for me to go back to the stairs.

I fold my arms and shake my head.

Her brows draw together.

So do mine.

She waves me off dismissively before tiptoeing toward the back of the house.

I'd rather run to the front door and escape, but I'm not going anywhere alone. There's too much space between here and there. And I know how dangerous the curved staircase can be if someone wants to cause bodily harm.

As we near the backside of the house, we pass several closed rooms. Most of which we've yet to go into at all. So much of this place is shrouded in mystery. And the air back here is chillier. Has a bit of a stale odor, despite how often she opens the windows.

Creak!

I nearly jump out of my skin.

Kenzi keeps going as if nothing just sounded.

I hurry to catch up with her. She peeks into the few rooms that are actually open. Grandma's old workout room. A smaller library Grandpa always called a den filled with old portraits, not unlike the photos we were just looking at upstairs. An old playroom with ancient toys that belong in a museum—a room that would scare the life out of me if I went into it in the dark.

We go all the way to the staircase leading to the downstairs.

My aunt looks at me, says nothing.

I want to say something, but my mind is racing. I couldn't possibly spit out a coherent thought.

She gestures toward the stairs.

Good. We're on the same page. Time to get outside. And fast.

We lean on the carved railing and make our way down. Some of the stairs creak under our weight. They always protest, but this time it seems louder than normal. Like they're shouting our location to whomever closed us into the third floor.

When we make it to the bottom, my aunt doesn't race for the door like a sane person. No, she goes to the left, heading toward the basement and the entrance to the tunnel.

"Have you lost your mind?" I whisper.

Her only response is to shake her head.

I should run outside, but I can't leave her alone in here when she could face a ghost or a robber. We pass more closed doors. Open ones, too. The dance hall would be the perfect place to hide. Thankfully, Kenzi doesn't go inside.

As we pass the door to the basement, she slows. Stares. Her hands shake. Then she quickly hurries away. I definitely have to ask her about why it freaks her out so bad, and I will if we survive this. Otherwise, it doesn't matter.

We both stare at the full-length mirror as we pass. My aunt keeps going, but I stop.

"Wait!"

She turns and gives me a questioning look.

"It's cracked open."

"What?" Kenzi backtracks and her mouth falls open. "You didn't do that, did you?"

"No. I swear."

She mutters under her breath.

"I take it you didn't, either?"

"No." My aunt moves the table aside, pulls out her phone, opens the door, and shines her light down the stairs.

"See anything?" I whisper.

"Nothing." She closes it, then we both push the table back to where it belongs.

"Aren't we going to install a lock?"

"The locksmith is coming out Friday. I couldn't get her here earlier."

"She came out pretty fast when we needed the locks on our main doors changed."

"It was an emergency. I think the detective might've pulled some strings."

The detective again. She keeps mentioning him. Why is he so involved in our case? Because our house has so many rumors about it? Or something else entirely?

Not that there's time to question her. She's already heading down the hallway.

We stop at the main library and look around.

Empty.

Then we continue on, passing closed doors—I wonder if we

shouldn't check out those rooms too—until we come to Grandpa's office. Nothing unusual in there.

We're almost to the front door. To freedom.

I start to relax. We just have to get past the kitchen. Then I'm racing outside no matter what my aunt decides to do.

She stops at the entrance. Pokes her head in.

Screams.

My heart skips a beat. I reach for a wall to balance myself. Manage to get my feet to move.

Look in the kitchen. Nearly pass out.

Someone is eating at the table.

23

Kenzi

My mind goes blank as I stare at the figure sitting at the table, back to us. I have to be imagining this. At the same time, there's no way I am. Not given the ashen look on my niece's face.

This cannot be happening.

I step into the kitchen. "Mom?"

She turns around slowly, as if nothing is wrong with this picture. "Mackenzie."

Ember throws me a wide-eyed confused look.

I take a few unsteady steps toward my mother. "What are you doing here?"

"Eating lunch. I see you still eat crap. This stuff will kill you, I hope you know."

"How did you get in?"

"The back entrance." She turns back to the table.

I nearly laugh, except there's nothing funny about this situation. "You *have* been coming in through the tunnel?"

Her only response is to nod.

"Why are you here?"

"I can't very well stay in the home anymore, can I? Not now that my secret is known."

Ember takes heavy steps over to her. "Why did you fake dementia, Grandma? That's not funny, you know."

"I wasn't trying to be funny."

Silence settles between the three of us.

As the reality of the situation hits me, a range of emotions thunders through me—everything from anger to shock. "You've actually been sneaking into the house?"

My mother just nods as she continues eating.

"Why?" I demand.

"This is my house."

I march over. "Legally, it's mine."

"And it was in your father's name before that. Didn't make it any less my house."

"Actually, it was Claire's before mine."

Mom shrugs.

Ember gives me a wild expression.

I shake my head, having no answers, and sit across from my mother. My niece takes the seat next to me. Mom keeps eating like nothing is out of place.

"Did you try to lock us on the third floor?" I demand.

"Why would I do that?"

"Did you close the door?" I shout.

"Yes. It shouldn't be open."

I squeeze the table. "Did you happen to think that it was propped open for a reason?"

"There is no reason to keep it open. The third floor is the place where secrets go to die."

"That isn't all, is it?"

She sets her fork down. "What isn't?"

"Secrets aren't the only thing that have died up there, are they?"

Mom sighs dramatically. "I don't know what you're talking about."

"Really?"

"Really." She goes back to her lunch.

"How did you get here?"

"Must we discuss this now?"

"Yes!" I slam my palm on the table.

Both my mother and niece jump.

"Always so dramatic." Mom sips her water.

"Dramatic?" I exclaim. "If anything, I'm under-reacting!"

She sets down her glass. "If I hadn't spent nearly thirty hours in labor with you, I'd swear there was no way you were my child."

"I'll never hear the end of the thirty hours of labor, will I?"

"You'll understand if you ever have children. But you'll never mature to that stage of life, will you?"

I clench my fists. "Speaking of children, how many have you birthed?"

"It's none of your business."

"It very much is! How many siblings do I have?"

Her mouth forms a straight line. "None, now."

"How can you be so callous?"

"I'm not. It's the simple truth. You have no living siblings."

"Did you mourn Claire at all?"

"Of course I did! Made all the worse because I had to hide it from everyone."

"Since you were living a lie." I cross one leg over the other and stare her down.

"I was doing what I needed in order to survive."

I snort. "You had to fake memory loss to *survive*?"

"Yes. Richard was going to kill me. I could see it in his eyes."

"He was going to kill you? That's a strong accusation."

"Don't act surprised. He always despised me but couldn't do a thing because of your father. Once he was gone, there was nothing holding him back." She gets up and collects her plate and silverware. "Do you two want something to eat?"

"Something to eat?"

"That's what I asked."

I exchange an incredulous look with my niece. "You can't just walk in here and act like everything is fine! Start making us lunch like the last five years never happened."

She puts the plates into the dishwasher and turns back to me. "We all know I have my full faculties. You two look like you've just been wrestling in the dirt, so let me fix you something. We can talk while I cook."

Ember lifts a brow. "Grandma, why don't you just tell us what's going on? Forget about food and start at the beginning."

"Cookies?" Mom asks. "Or do you want a cake?"

I rise. "We don't want to eat anything! All we want is answers."

"I'll talk, but I'd be happier making something to eat. Perhaps you'd prefer dinner. I could make lasagna. You might be hungry by the time that's done, and I'm pretty sure you have most of the ingredients." She opens the refrigerator. "Enough that I can make do, anyway." She glances at me. "Someone really needs to teach you how to shop, especially now that you're raising my granddaughter."

"We've been getting by just fine."

"I hope you're at least taking vitamins. You need to make up for your poor nutrition somewhere." She places meat onto the counter.

"Not that I need to defend myself to you, but we have plenty of green smoothies."

"Smoothies." She makes a face then continues digging through the fridge.

Ember throws me a confused look.

I shrug, hardly able to believe the situation. But here we are, and I have to figure out what to do. Get to the bottom of what's really going on. Has my mother been sneaking into the house ever since we moved in? Longer? Ever since she was committed?

She hums as she begins cooking the meat.

I lean against the counter. "How long have you been sneaking in here?"

"What do you mean?" She sprinkles spices onto the meat.

"When did you start sneaking in here? Just recently, or all five years?"

"I'd rather talk about something else. Hand me the noodles."

I glare at her but do as she asks. "We need to discuss this. Then we have to get you back to the retirement home after this little field trip."

"Oh, I've been checked out. My time there is done."

"What? They just let you go? No paperwork? What about your things? I can't believe they'd do that without informing me first!"

"Your permission isn't necessary. I'm a fully functioning adult." She opens the oven and looks in before closing it. "And technically, nobody was placed as my guardian after Claire's death. I was completely overlooked." She glances at me. "Don't look at me like that. I expected that, and it worked in my favor."

"This is unbelievable. You can't live here!"

"Why not?" My mother stirs the meat and adds more spices. "This has been my home for half a century."

"Not for the last five years, it hasn't."

"Only to keep me safe."

I bite my tongue to keep from asking what I really want to ask, but can't yet—why were her prints on that knife upstairs and whose blood was all over that room?

Ember steps over to where we are. "Safe from what, Grandma?"

"Your horrible stepfather."

"What was he going to do to you?"

"Kill me, like I said."

Ember's brows furrow. "But what made you think that?"

"He told me as much, dear." Mom pours salt into the boiling water.

My niece's eyes widen. "He *told* you he was going to kill you?"

"He did." She stirs the meat again and lowers the heat.

I lean against the counter. "Why didn't you call the police? Speak with Claire?"

"Richard became best friends with the old captain. The man could get away with anything. Well, almost anything. I'm glad to see murder wasn't actually on that list. How was I to know?"

I rub my temples. "What's going on now? Your plan is to live here?"

"Yes." She picks up a box of frozen asparagus. "Fresh vegetables are so much healthier than frozen."

"You can do the shopping from here on out. Problem solved." I pour myself a glass of wine even though I want something much stronger.

Mom glances at my glass. "I should've offered you two something to drink."

"Ember's too young for alcohol, Mom."

"I didn't mean hard drinks, Mackenzie."

"I go by Kenzi."

"But that's not your name. I should know—I gave it to you."

"You and Dad did."

She shrugs and puts the asparagus in a pan.

I finish my wine. "Tell us about the tunnel. How long have you been using it?"

"Many years. Since I was a young lady."

"Did Dad know?"

"Of course not. I don't think he even knew it existed."

Ember and I exchange another glance.

"What did you use it for back then?" I ask.

She wrinkles her forehead. "What do you think? It's never been easy being married to such a powerful man. You think Richard got away with a lot—that's nothing compared to the man whose bloodline started this town. Everyone always thought I was so lucky to marry into such wealth, but nobody ever considered what it was like to be under the thumb of the Brannon men."

"Men?" I lift a brow. "As in, plural?"

"Yes, dear. Your grandfather lived a long life, and we mustn't forget Jack."

"Jack? Which one?"

"Your uncle." She removes the meat from the stove.

"He's dead."

"But he wasn't always."

I rub my temples. "He died as a boy."

"No. He died *young*. In his twenties. Though given the way people act nowadays, that could still be considered a boy."

I hold back an eye roll. "So, you knew Uncle Jack?"

"Yes. I lived here in this house with all three of the Brannon men. Let me tell you, this place felt tiny with those tyrants all under one roof."

"Grandpa wasn't a tyrant!" Ember stomps a foot.

"Not to you girls, no."

"What are you saying?" I ask.

"He treated you girls like gold."

I snort. "You seem to forget I couldn't do a thing right by either one of you. That's the reason I fled to LA."

She holds my gaze a moment before speaking. "You always were the smart one."

It's a good thing I'm done with my wine, or it would go right up my nose. "Me? Yeah, right. You know better than that—you complained about my grades more than anyone else."

"You could've done a lot better if you'd tried. We all know that."

Ember lifts a brow.

"I don't want to talk about my grades right now. Stop circling the topics. How did you get released from the home? And how did you get here?"

She takes a deep breath. "I already told you. I'm of sound mind—they can't hold me."

"I mean, how did you get inside?"

"We already established that. I went through the tunnel. I've been using it for decades."

"Why didn't you knock? Ring the bell? Call me?"

"I did all three. No answer. So, I went around back and came through the one way I knew I could get in without a key."

"How'd you call me?" I ask. "My phone didn't ring."

"The man who drove me called."

"Doesn't explain my phone not ringing."

"You were upstairs, right?" she asks.

"Yeah. What does that have to do with anything?"

"The cell signals have always jammed up there."

I tilt my head. "You'd know that how?"

"Because I've lived here most of my life. Check your phone."

To humor her, I pull out my phone. Sure enough, it shows a missed call when Ember and I were on the third floor. I also have a message from Dayton.

"Am I right?" Mom looks like she's trying not to smirk.

"You know my number off the top of your head?"

She taps her temple. "I have a memory like a steel trap. You've had the same number since you got your first phone."

I take a deep breath. "Where's your luggage?"

"I have one suitcase. It's underneath the main staircase. You probably didn't see it because it's tucked away so well."

My head is spinning. I pinch the top of my nose, not that it helps. "And you just signed yourself out of the facility?"

She nods. "That place is for people with severe memory issues."

I mull over the deception. "What about the medication?"

"What do you think? I spit them out when nobody was looking." Mom looks proud of herself.

"How'd you get in, in the first place? Into the facility, I mean."

"It was easy. I always dreamed of being an actress. If I hadn't married your father, that's what I would've done. I'd have gone to Hollywood and made a name for myself."

"*You* wanted to go to California?"

"Who do you think planted that idea in your mind, Mackenzie?"

"Kenzi! Call me Kenzi."

"I don't know why you'd choose to butcher such a pretty name, but okay. I'll call you Kenzi, if that'll make you happy."

"Thank you," I say through gritted teeth. "What makes you think you planted the idea of Cali in my head?"

She takes the boiling pasta off the stove and turns to me. "When you were little, we used to talk about how fun it would be to go there and act. We made up stories about what kinds of movies we'd be in, and how much fun it would be. Even though you don't remember the conversations, clearly they made an impact. And you're still acting up here?"

"I suppose you could call it that. It's hardly as glamorous as you'd have wanted for yourself."

"But you're happy with it?"

"Yeah. It's a lot of fun."

"Good. That's what matters."

I just stare at her. Who *is* this woman?

24

Kenzi

I close my eyes but can't sleep. I've been trying but it's fruitless. There are a thousand more questions I have for my mother, but it got too late to ask them all. After we ate dinner, she claimed she was too tired and wanted to go to bed. And before that, she wanted to know about our lives and wouldn't answer any more questions about herself.

She's staying in the largest guest room, which is at the back of the second floor, about as far away from Ember and me as possible. The room had originally been used for the most important houseguests, and many times held large families. It's almost as big as the master bedroom, which is now mine.

Mom had said she wouldn't take it even if we'd left it as it had been when it'd been hers and Dad's. She claimed it held too many bad memories. The more she spoke openly about Dad, the more clear it became how much she despised not only him but also his father and brother. She kept referring to them as the Brannon men and had a scowl each time she said that.

After dinner, I called the facility and confirmed her story.

She was no longer a resident, and the owner himself had dropped her off at the house—but obviously hadn't stuck around long enough to make sure she got inside.

Given the entire stunt my mother had pulled, I couldn't help but wonder if the owner was in on her plan from the beginning. Why he would be was anyone's guess. Though I'm sure it had to do with money. As Mom had basically said herself, Brannon money got people all kinds of favors.

And now that she's back here, I don't know what to think. How did her prints get on that knife upstairs? Did she actually kill someone? If so, who? And when? It had to have been a long time ago, given the thick layer of dust in the room. Nothing had been touched up there in the decades before Ember found everything. Her pictures proved as much. The dust hadn't been disturbed until she went up.

Beyond that, I also want to know how the two Jacks died. Mom *did* know Dad's brother. He hadn't died in childhood. He'd been in his twenties. Was it his blood on the knife? How did my brother die? Or is he still alive somewhere? I don't know why he would be, given he'd have had to walk away from family and the inheritance. Unless, like me, he just wanted to get away from the insanity. Maybe he didn't live up to the high Brannon family expectations.

What if we now have a killer living with us? Did she kill in self-defense? Or had it been something more sinister? It was hard to believe anything that came from her mouth considering she'd spent the last five years faking dementia.

It was obvious where I got my acting skills from. At least I used mine for good. I don't know what to think about her. For all Ember and I know, she's still putting on a performance. Everything she told us could've been lies. Except I know what she said about the facility is true. The rest of it is one big question mark.

I fling off my covers and sit up. How am I supposed to sleep knowing a killer could be living with us? I get up and tiptoe to Ember's room.

Knock, knock.

"Come in."

I open the door and find her lounging on her bed, typing on her laptop. "Can't sleep?"

She closes it quickly. "Nope."

"What do you think about your grandma being here?"

"It's weird. I mean, I guess it's good, but it's strange. She's been lying about the memory loss this whole time? Mom and I used to visit her, and she never once gave us a clue."

"You don't know why Richard might want her dead?"

Ember shrugs. "Because he's a jerk?"

"Can't argue with that." I take a deep breath. "Do you feel safe with her here?"

"Why wouldn't I?"

I don't bring up the knife. No point in scaring her if I don't have to.

She lifts a brow.

"At least now when we hear strange noises at night, we know it's probably her. We had no clue she was coming here through that tunnel."

"Still doesn't explain everything," Ember says.

"Such as?"

"The little girl giggling." She gives me a knowing look.

"That could be explained by a lot of things."

Ember yawns. "We can talk about that later. I need to get some sleep. Gretchen wants to go to the beach tomorrow with some kids from school."

"Oh, good." I give her a hug. "I'm so glad you're getting together with friends more."

"I wouldn't really call the others friends."

"Why not?"

She groans. "Like I said, I'm tired. Goodnight."

"Goodnight." I get up and close the door behind me, then make my way down the hall to Mom's new room.

The light is on, and shadows move under her door.

I'm tempted to knock but don't want to get sucked into a conversation. Like my niece, I need some sleep. I have another lunch date tomorrow outside of town. Part of me wants to stay and keep an eye on my mom, but the sane part of me wants to be as far away from her as I can get.

Back in my room, I close the door and flop back onto the bed. A spring digs into my side, reminding me I promised Ember we could both get new furniture for our rooms. I scoot over and look at my phone.

I never checked the message Dayton sent. Maybe he wants to discuss our Thanksgiving date. It's a way off still—it's only August—but he's mentioned it numerous times when we've seen or spoken with each other.

I check the message. He asks about a date, but much sooner than November.

Dayton: My family is persuasive. I'm actually considering a branch of my business up in Seattle and have another luncheon scheduled next week. Are you willing to have another meal with my family? They really like you. If you're up for it, let me know and we can discuss the details.

I have to re-read the message twice to make sure I'm seeing it right. But I am. He actually wants another date with me.

Now I have two regular clients, when before I rarely had a repeat customer. Actually, given the earlier coffee date with Graham, I'm not sure what to label us. I had thought we'd be meeting while he was on the clock, but he's on vacation and he kept putting his hand on top of mine and looking at me the way he did.

It doesn't matter. I'm not looking for anything serious. That's the last thing I need. It's also the last thing either one of them want, so I don't know why I'm getting freaked out.

Graham probably only had his hand on mine to be friendly. Friends do that.

Then why is my face warming? Not that it matters. My life is crazy enough without adding in the drama of actual dates.

I send Dayton a quick message to let him know I'd love to see his family again.

The dancing dots indicate he's responding already.

I want to ask what he's doing up so late, but that would be getting too personal. He probably works late. Long hours. One of those guys who has a setup so he can sleep in the office to save time. Not that it's any of my business.

Dayton: Great news. I'll contact the agency to set up the details. See you soon.

Kenzi: Sounds like a plan. Goodnight.

Dayton: Pleasant dreams.

I stare at those two words. They seem a bit too personal. Or is it a typical British response to goodnight? I'm probably making too big a deal of this, blowing things out of proportion because I'm trying to process everything my mother has said since she showed up.

What I need is to get some rest. Everything will look different in the morning.

I hope.

Not that anything will have changed. My mom, who is capable of living a lie for years on end, is now back in the house. And I have no idea what her angle is.

25

Ember

My heart is still racing. I can't believe I almost let Kenzi see what I was doing on my computer. If I were smart, I'd have closed the laptop before she came in, but I thought she was just going to check on me. I didn't expect her to sit down and try to have a heart-to-heart with me.

I glance at my door for what has to be the fiftieth time. She must've gone to bed. I really don't want her to know what I'm doing. I'm not even sure I want to go down that path. But so far, I'm just looking. No harm in that.

Especially considering I'm not finding anything.

I reopen my laptop and stare at the search in front of me. There are a surprising amount of Grahams in the eastern states, especially the south. Must be a popular name there. Or at least more popular than here. I've never even met one.

If only my mom had gotten more information about him. But I can't blame her. It wasn't like she thought he was going to father her child. It was just supposed to be a one-time encounter. She wasn't expecting to get me out of it.

I also can't find Sasha Beckett, the friend who brought Mom to the party where she met my dad. Sasha probably got married and has a new last name, which makes her just as hard to find as my biological father. All I have is first names. It would help if Mom was connected to a Sasha or a Graham on social media, but nope. Neither one. Not connected to a Sasha or a Graham on any of her accounts.

I should be grateful to at least have found the note she left me. If I hadn't been in Mom's childhood room and accidentally knocked those papers over, I wouldn't even have this much.

I'm tempted to try one of those DNA tests where you spit into a tube and find out about your ancestry. But what if my dad hasn't done one of those? Then I'd end up with nothing. Or what if he has?

My heart races at the thought. I don't know what scares me more—the thought of finding him or the thought of *not* finding him. The prospect that he would want to know me or that he wouldn't.

It's the unknown I hate.

Crash!

I jump. Nearly knock my computer off the bed. Manage to catch it before it drops.

My pulse drums in my ears. I shouldn't be surprised by the sound. Now Grandma can make all the noise she wants. No more sneaking around required.

I should probably check to see if she's okay. What if she fell? I shudder, picturing her taking a tumble down the stairs. But that didn't happen. It was just one crash, not a series of them. I wait, not hearing anything else.

She probably just knocked something over. She's been busy rearranging her new bedroom.

But I can't let go of the thought that she might've hurt herself. She is used to other people taking care of her, even if she's been capable the whole time. Now she's out of her element. Or is she right back in it? It's so hard to say. This whole thing is just weird—my grandma has been faking her memory loss all this time, and now she's acting like everything is totally normal.

I don't even know her, if I'm being totally honest. It's been five years since she was normal—or at least since we all thought she was. I was ten. That was so long ago. Almost feels like a lifetime. Actually, more. My life has been split into two parts, when Mom was alive and since her death. My chest squeezes at the thought. It's painful to think about, and sometimes it really hits me hard when I least expect it. I like to keep myself busy and distracted so I don't have to deal with how hard it is.

And checking on Grandma is exactly what I need right now. Mom would want me to watch out for her. That's what I'm going to do.

What if the crash was her hurting herself?

I set my laptop on the desk, tiptoe to the door, slowly open it, and go out into the hall. Everything is quiet, dim. Something creaks in the distance. I don't know where, it's barely noticeable.

I release a breath I didn't realize I was holding and creep toward the room Grandma is now staying in. My skin crawls. I slow my pace, listening. Nothing sounds other than my soft footsteps. If I didn't know better, I'd think I was in a normal house. But I'm not, and I'm not letting my guard down.

Once I turn down the hall toward Grandma's room, darkness envelops me. There are no nightlights because Kenzi and I don't go this way at night.

I make a mental note to add nightlights to the shopping list.

Holding my breath, I trail my fingertips along the wall and follow the hall by memory and feel. I wish I'd brought my phone for light, but I hadn't been thinking like that. Next time.

No. Next time, there will be nightlights. Maybe enough to

make every path in the entire house lit at night. Or at least on the two main levels. I can't imagine us having any reason to go anywhere else at night. I definitely don't have any desire.

My pulse keeps racing faster with each step I take. I'm getting nearer to Grandma's room, but I have no idea how close I am. It's so dark. No windows to let in any light.

A scuffling noise sounds in front of me. Like feet running, lightly.

I freeze in place and listen, suddenly aware of how vulnerable I am. Can't see anything around me. Darkness surrounds me, hiding me from the world. I try to say something, but my voice won't cooperate.

This was dumb. I never should have come down this hallway. Not without a light, but I hadn't thought about that. I take a deep breath and keep going.

I'm also almost to Grandma's room. I have to be. Just a little farther, then I'll check on her and race back to my room. To light, to safety. Not that I'm unsafe here. The entire house is protected with the alarm system. Well, except the mirror-door. We're still waiting on the locksmith for that. But who else knows about that? And now we know where Grandma is, and that she won't be sneaking through the door.

I turn again, and this time a little light comes into view. It's coming from underneath her door. It isn't much, but it's something. I can see, and now I have something to aim for. Once I see she's okay and prove I've gotten myself worked up over nothing, I can get back to my bed and go to sleep. Perfect plan.

The hairs on the back of my neck rise as I near the door. I ignore them and the gooseflesh forming on my arms. There isn't anything unusual here. I'm just walking in the hallway of my house to check on my grandma. That's all.

Music sounds from the other side of the doorway. I try to place it. It's upbeat but different from anything I listen to. Probably something from one of those old programs she likes to watch.

Though I can't help but wonder if that wasn't all just for show.

I hesitate before knocking, try to place the music because it's a good distraction. Then I ball my fist to knock but wait. Maybe I should go in rather than knocking. I'm curious what she does when nobody's looking.

It's hard to imagine someone who could pull off such a façade for so long, yet my own flesh and blood had managed it for five long years. What else was she capable of?

I reach for the knob, but then guilt pricks. Despite what she's done, she deserves privacy, respect. I'd want that much. Not that I'd ever pull a stunt like she did, tricking my kids and grandkids.

Knock, knock.

The music stops, and shuffling noises sound from inside the room. The light under the door shifts as she makes her way toward me.

My breath hitches. I don't know what I expect to see.

The door opens, the light nearly blinding me, and she appears wearing a fuzzy pink bathrobe and curlers in her hair. "Ember. Is everything okay, dear?"

"I just came to check on you."

"Don't trust me?"

"That's not it." I answer too quickly. "I heard something crash, and I was worried you'd hurt yourself."

She scratches her head. "A crash?"

I nod.

"I didn't hear anything."

"Your music was pretty loud."

She glances around. "Was it disturbing you?"

"No. I can't hear it from my room. But I did hear a noise. You sure you didn't drop anything? It would've been a few minutes ago."

"Can't say that anything fell in here. Must've been Macken—Kenzi. Her room is much closer to yours than mine."

"You could always stay in one closer to us. Then we could all watch out for each other."

"Oh, this one is fine. I've always wanted to have this room, but your grandfather insisted on the other one. Why, I don't know. This one is equally as big. The only difference is that the heads of the house have always used that other room." She shrugs. "Brannon men and their insistence on following family traditions. I'll never understand it, but I suppose it doesn't matter any longer, now does it?"

"I guess not." I try to look around her to see what she's done to the room.

Grandma steps aside. "Do you want to have a look around? Can't say there's much to see yet. It'll take a lot more time than one evening."

"Um, sure."

I step inside, trying to remember what it looked like before. There are so many rooms, it's hard to keep them all straight. I'm pretty sure this was one that was still covered in sheets and plastic. Now all that has been removed to reveal what looks like a hotel suite, but with antique furniture, like so much else in this house. If I remember correctly, it had been a guest room for visiting families, though everyone would've had to share the enormous bed. It *looks* big enough to fit a big group of people.

Grandma moves in front of an armoire and closes it, standing in front of it. "I don't have a lot to work with. Just the one suitcase I was allowed at the home and what's left of my things that your aunt didn't get rid of. She was pretty eager to erase me from that room."

"That wasn't what Kenzi was doing. What's in there?"

Grandma's expression tenses, and I notice that she's applied makeup and shaped her brows. "No?" she asks. "What do you call it, then, when my daughter got rid of my things?"

"Making the room into hers. Just like I've been doing with her old room."

Grandma sighs. "She got rid of a lot of things."

"We both did," I say in Kenzi's defense. "This place was a huge mess, and there's so much to go through. Most stuff has stayed, but we did have to throw some things out."

"More than some. Not that it matters. We're all here together now. That's what matters."

My back stiffens. "We're not *all* here."

She shakes her head. "Poor Claire. I never saw that coming. I'd have stopped her murder if I could have."

"How come you were concerned only about yourself?"

"Pardon me?" Grandma stands taller.

"Why was your concern only for *you*? You knew he was dangerous, yet you did nothing to protect either me or my mom. Instead of saying anything to us, or even letting us know what your real plan was, you faked dementia and allowed us to think you forgot us."

"It had to be done—and like I said, I didn't think he'd do anything to you two."

"You didn't say that."

She rubs her temples. "It's been a long day. Why don't we continue this conversation tomorrow? It's going to be morning soon, and we both need our sleep. I can't tell you how nice it'll be to sleep without the disruptions of the other patients."

"You didn't have to live like that."

Her mouth forms a straight line. "You don't understand."

"That's one thing you have right." I spin around to exit the room, but first I turn back to her. "I'm glad you're safe. Kenzi and I have your best interests in mind. I hope you have our backs."

Grandma's eyes widen. She doesn't respond.

Sighing, I close the door between us. Then I feel the wall until I get back to the main part of the second floor and have the nightlights guiding my way again.

What secrets is she hiding? And what didn't she want me to see in the armoire?

26

Ember

The smell of bacon wakes me. For a moment, I think I'm back home and Mom must be making a weekend break-fast. On the rare occasions she didn't work, she made elaborate breakfasts for the two of us. Richard was rarely there, as he was always working.

But reality hits me almost as soon as I think of Mom's cooking. She'll never make another breakfast again. No more of her special chocolate pancakes or fruit and whipped cream-covered waffles.

Never again.

The thought of that makes me want to stay in bed all day and feel sorry for myself. Luckily, I don't have to work at the art camp this week, so I *could* make myself stay home under the covers. But Gretchen wants to go to the beach today, and she'll drag me kicking and screaming if she has to. Plus, it would do me good to get out of this house and away from the craziness. And I definitely need more sun. The popular girls will start calling me a vampire if I don't tan soon. Not that I care what they think.

My stomach rumbles and I force myself out of bed. The sun is shining brightly, lighting up the room. If I didn't know better, I'd never guess how creepy this place is at night.

I'm tempted to get a shower before heading downstairs, but that can wait. I mean seriously, bacon.

A glimpse of my reflection in the mirror makes me jolt. My hair is standing out in all directions and I have dark circles under my eyes—not surprising given how long it took me to fall asleep last night.

I pull my hair back and dab a little coverup underneath my eyes. Just enough to make sure my aunt or grandma don't start to worry. Though I have to wonder if Grandma would notice or care. When I was little, she fussed over me. But that was before living a lie and not even letting us in on what was really going on.

It's hard not to wonder what Mom would've thought of all this. She didn't get mad often, but something like this would definitely set her off. We all really believed Grandma had forgotten everything and everyone. But it was all a sham to hide from Richard. This is definitely going to take some digging.

I'm going to get to the bottom of this one way or another.

But first, bacon.

My stomach rumbles, and I head downstairs. It's even brighter in the main part of the house where there are so many windows to let in the summer's morning light.

Conversation sounds from the kitchen. Not surprising. Grandma and Kenzi are probably talking about the tunnel or another of Grandma's many secrets.

But then I hear a male voice. I freeze mid-step. A guy is here?

I strain to hear the conversation but can't make out any

words. Only tones, and one of the people talking is definitely a dude.

I look down at my choice of sleepwear. Tiny polka-dotted shorts and a camisole. Hardly appropriate to wear in front of some guy. I hurry upstairs and slip into a loose but light hoodie and some capri pajama pants. It'll have to do. Hopefully, it isn't someone young and cute. If they invited Luke in, the kid who delivers our groceries, I would die of embarrassment.

Maybe a shower isn't such a bad idea.

But my stomach rumbles, convincing me to go downstairs as I am. Surely, Kenzi would warn me if a hot guy was downstairs. Even if she didn't, it wouldn't be the end of the world. That's what he gets for coming over so early.

I make myself go down the stairs again. As I creep along the hall, I realize I recognize the male voice. Can't place it, but it is familiar. Makes me more curious and offers relief—it's not Luke.

When I enter the kitchen, I don't immediately see our guest. Grandma stands at the stove, flipping over a sausage. My aunt must be at the table with the dude.

Grandma turns to me and smiles brightly. "You finally woke. Are you hungry?"

"Yeah, thanks." I head over to the Keurig machine and make myself a cup, not bothering to put anything in it. It's a black coffee kind of a morning. I take a few sips before turning around.

When I do, Grandma hands me a full plate.

Even with as hungry as I am, I doubt I can eat that much.

"Eat up," she says. "You need more meat on your bones."

"She's fine," Kenzi says.

"Thank you." I sit next to her and study the familiar man on the other side of her. It feels like I should know who he is, but I don't.

"Morning, Ember." He nods.

Great. He knows my name.

"Hi." I sit and take a bite of bacon.

Kenzi turns to me. "You remember Detective Felton?"

Suddenly, everything comes back to me. I don't know why I didn't recognize him before. Maybe it's the plain clothes that threw me. But then, I think he wore a leather jacket before, so that doesn't explain it. Probably the stress of everything. I was dealing with my mom's death when I'd seen him before. I nod to him. "Yeah. Hi. Everything okay?"

"Just came to see the tunnel your aunt was telling me about."

"Oh?"

"We were concerned about its safety."

I pick up another piece of bacon. "Were? You're not anymore?"

"I still am, but the fact that your grandmother has been using it all this time puts my mind at ease. Although I would like to check it out to be sure. Originally, I was going to bring a crew. Might still, depending on how it looks."

I glance at Kenzi. "Are we going to check it out too?"

"I am. I want to see it for myself."

"So do I."

She and the detective exchange a glance.

"You aren't going to let me, are you?"

My aunt gives me an apologetic expression. "Once we know it's safe, you can have a look. I don't want to put you in danger."

I turn to Grandma. "Is the tunnel dangerous?"

"Not at all. Whoever built it knew what they were doing. There are support beams all throughout. It could survive an earthquake—and in fact, it has. We've had many over the years, and the tunnel hasn't suffered a bit."

"See?" I glance at Kenzi. "It's fine."

"We'll be the judge."

The detective straightens his back and pushes the chair out. "Actually, I'm going to do a walk-through first."

My aunt's mouth drops open. "What?"

I stifle a giggle.

He nods. "I'm waiting for my partner, then we'll have a look. If anything appears dangerous, we'll turn around."

Kenzi frowns. "You have to follow protocol?"

"There's hardly protocol for how to explore a secret tunnel, but this is how our captain thinks we should proceed."

"But my mom, an elderly and frail woman, has been going back and forth for ..." Her voice trails off then she turns to Grandma. "How long have you been using the tunnel?"

"That depends. Who are you calling elderly and frail?"

"How long?" Kenzi's brows draw together.

"Long enough."

"That doesn't tell us anything."

Grandma shrugs. "What do you expect from a decrepit old lady?"

My aunt scowls. "That isn't what I said."

Instead of responding, Grandma fills the sink with dishes and soap.

"When did you discover it?" asks the detective.

"Years ago."

"How many? An estimate?"

"When my husband was still alive."

Kenzi sighs dramatically. "That's hardly helpful. You were sent to the facility after he passed. Obviously you'd have had to know about it to get in that way."

"I was *sent* there?"

My aunt turns to the detective. "We're not going to get anything out of her. I want to go through the tunnel when you do. This is my property."

She stares him down. It's like they're familiar with each other beyond the fact that he was looking into my mom's murder. Or maybe it's my imagination. My aunt is one of those people who just naturally gets on with people as soon as she meets them. I think it's because of her job. She has to be a pro at putting on an act to pretend to be the fiancée or best friend of someone she just met.

But given the look on the detective's face, I don't think her charisma is going to be enough to convince him to let her explore with him.

Grandma turns, her eyes narrowed.

The detective shakes his head. "That may be, but it's still a matter of safety."

Kenzi turns her attention back to Grandma. "How did you discover the tunnel? If Dad didn't know about it, how did you?"

Grandma doesn't respond right away.

"Mom?" My aunt sounds irritated.

"It was your uncle. He showed me."

"Uncle Jack? Why?"

"He wanted privacy."

"Privacy?" She exchanges a confused glance with Felton. "For what?"

Ding-dong!

He pushes his chair back. "My partner is here."

Kenzi leaps up. "Doesn't mean I can't go with you guys." She turns to Grandma. "We'll continue this discussion later."

"You can stay at the entrance." The detective marches into the hall toward the front door.

My aunt turns to me. "*You* can stay at the entrance."

If nothing else, this will be interesting.

27

Kenzi

I step down onto the first rickety step. Then the next.

Ember follows me. "You go, I go."

I stop and glance back. "You heard the detective. Someone needs to stand at the entrance. What if something goes wrong?"

"He told you to wait for them to come back."

"It's also been a full ten minutes since we last heard from them."

"Then use that walkie-talkie thing he gave you. It goes both ways."

I can't argue with that. "Aren't you supposed to be getting ready for the beach?"

"This is more interesting."

I try to use the device in my hand to call Graham, but I can't find the right button. If only my phone would work, but there's no signal in the tunnel. I already tried. "Back up. I need light to work this thing."

My niece moves back, and I join her in the hallway, my eyes

readjusting to the light. I manage to find the right button to reach the detective.

"Felton," he answers.

Relief washes through me at the sound of his voice. "How's it going?"

"Everything still looks good."

"Are you near the end?"

He chuckles. "No way to know until we get there."

"Let me know."

"Will do."

I put the radio back. "Where's Mom? She should've been back by now."

"Probably organizing her room or cooking." Ember leans against the door and sighs.

"You okay?"

She nods then yawns.

"Getting enough sleep?"

"Can you ask some more questions?"

"I'm trying to be helpful." I crane my neck to try and see down the hall. Cup my ears but don't hear anything.

"She's probably scaring the ghosts." Ember peeks into the tunnel entrance.

The corners of my mouth twitch. "I wouldn't put it past her, but in all seriousness, I need to check on her."

"She isn't a kid."

"Right. She's worse." I hand her the radio unit. "You know how to work this?"

"Yeah."

"If Felton gives you *any* update, call me." I pat my pocket where my phone is. "Okay?"

"Sure." Ember leans against the wall again. "I'm sure absolutely nothing will happen."

"Let's hope." I head down the hall, giving her another reminder over my shoulder to call me if she hears anything.

"Already said I would."

I peek in the kitchen as I pass. Empty. Then I make my way upstairs. Quiet, sunny. I head toward Mom's room, and the light dims as I move away from the large windows. Still no noises.

Except a child's giggle.

I ignore it. It's probably all in my head, anyway. Just being in this house—especially now, with my mom back here too—old dusty memories are being awoken. And my niece is right. If there are ghosts, they would be more frightened of my mom than the other way around.

Mom's door is closed. I rap my knuckles on the wood. "Mom? Are you in there?"

No response.

Maybe she's gotten into the habit of napping, though it's still pretty early.

I knock again, then warn her that I'm coming in. The room is dim with the curtains drawn. Nearly everything has been rearranged. She isn't anywhere to be seen.

Where would she be? Could be anywhere.

Then a thought strikes me. What if she went to my room? It had been hers for so many years. A sense of violation runs through me as I picture her rifling through my things. If she wouldn't have lied about her mental state, she would still have her room. She'd have been here in the house all this time.

Why would anyone choose to live in a memory care facility, pretending to have forgotten everything?

That's something I'll have to try to understand later. For now, I just need to find her in this enormous house. I make my way through the halls, my gaze lingering on each closed door. How many secrets remain hidden behind those? More than I have time to look into at the moment while I have a living, breathing mystery to solve.

When I get to my room, I peek in. Nothing is out of place. "Mom?"

Silence. Not even a giggle. I don't know whether to be relieved or worried.

I hurry over to the entrance to the third floor and call up. "Mom? Are you up there?"

Nothing.

This is taking too long. I check my phone. Nothing from Ember. I send her a text.

Kenzi: How's it going?

Ember: They're still exploring. Not at end yet.

Kenzi: Still?

Ember: Yep. Find Gma?

Kenzi: Not yet.

Ember: Serious?

Kenzi: LMK if u hear anything.

Ember: OK. U2.

My mind races. How long is that tunnel? I hadn't expected it to take half this long. The crazy part is that someone—or many someones—had to build it. Secretly, at that. Shorter makes more sense, right? Or did they think it would be better to go on for an insanely long way?

Knowing what I do about my ancestors, they didn't dig it themselves. They hired people who more than likely stayed up on the third floor. It had to have been for a long time if the tunnel really went as long as it seemed. Unless Graham and his partner were taking their time, stopping to examine every little thing. Maybe that's it. Because aside from the time it took to construct, there's also the fact that my mother who is in her seventies, has been traveling it on a regular basis. I have a hard time picturing her in a super long tunnel, especially if she needed to get back to the facility after doing what she needed to *and* traveling underground both in and out.

My head spins trying to make sense of it all. I need to stop expecting things to be like they should. It's the Brannon family I'm dealing with. A huge house with more secrets than I can probably imagine. Even if I made it my full-time job to find every one, it would take years. I'd probably have to pass the baton onto Ember.

After I make my way through the first and second levels, not going into the closed off rooms, I return to my niece. She looks up from her phone. "Didn't find her?"

I shake my head. "No idea where she went."

"Did you look out front? She used to enjoy time in the garden."

"It's now just weeds."

She shrugs. "Where else would she be?"

I look around, trying to think of anywhere I might've missed. "That's what I'd like to know. It might be time to check out some of the other rooms."

Ember puts her phone in her pocket. "Are you serious?"

"Where else would she be? I'd still be searching if I'd checked every single room. It could take hours, considering how long some of them have been closed off. Probably need a dust mask before entering."

She tilts her head. "You didn't look in any when the locks were being replaced?"

"I peeked in a few, but I was also dealing with the security system installation and the—"

A noise sounds from the tunnel. Can't tell what it is. It's faint.

Ember and I exchange a wide-eyed glance.

I reach for the radio unit. "Are they coming back? Did they reach the end?"

She hands it to me. "They didn't say."

My heart thunders. What if there was a cave-in? Or something dangerous my mother didn't warn us about?

Another sound from the tunnel. Sounds kind of like a rumble. That could definitely be a cave-in.

I click the button on the radio. "Hello? Hello? Are you there?"

It makes noise like someone is going to respond, but nobody speaks.

I'm about ready to throw the unit back to my niece and bolt in there. But I try again. "Hello? Are you okay?"

More radio noise. Then what sounds like a voice, but I can't make out any words.

"I'm coming in!"

Static. Then a clear voice. "No."

"Graham!"

Ember stares at me, color draining from her face. "Did you say—"

"Graham!" I call again, ready to race underground.

She repeats his name.

The radio makes noise. "One of the walls collapsed."

My heart leaps into my throat. "What? Are you trapped? Hurt?"

Ember just keeps staring at me.

Static. "We're not trapped. My leg is buried in rubble."

"I'll be right there!"

"No!" His voice is strained, he has to be in pain. "Remember how I showed you to radio my sergeant?"

"Yes, but—"

"Do that, Kenzi. Whit should close by. He'll be knocking in minutes."

"But I'm closer! Graham!"

"Listen to me. Radio Whit. Will you do that for me?"

Pressure builds in my chest. It takes every ounce of my self-control not to race in there. "Okay. Yes, I'll tell him what's going on. Will he bring others?"

"He knows what to do. Over and out."

I start to radio the sergeant, but hesitate when I notice

Ember's even paler now and breathing heavily. "Do you need help too? Are you having an asthma attack?"

I'm not even aware of her having any medical conditions, but something is clearly going on.

She shakes her head. "Just get them help."

I call the sergeant and in less than two minutes, the doorbell rings. Ember looks like she needs the wall for support, so I race for the front door.

28

Kenzi

P ain squeezes my chest as I stare helplessly into the tunnel entrance. At this point, more police than I can count have come into the house and either into the tunnel or into the backyard to figure out where Graham and his partner are.

Ember and I are both struggling to breathe normally as we wait. My mother still hasn't shown herself. I want to find her and chew her out for it, but it could be for the best that she's not in the way. It would just be nice to have her keep me in the loop. Not only am I worried for Graham's safety and Ember's fragile state, but now I need to think about Mom on top of everything else.

Once this is over, we're going to have to set some ground rules. It's weird, taking on the parenting role over my mother, but it's clearly necessary.

Whit steps out from the tunnel, dirt smeared across his face and weaved into his hair.

I leap over to him. "Are they okay?"

He wipes his eyes. "Yes. Felton will need that leg looked at, but he'll be fine. Might need some stitches."

I cringe. "It's that bad?"

Whit radios for a medic unit, and my heart sinks. I should have never told Graham about the tunnel. I'm glad I didn't bring Ember in there, at least. I'd have never forgiven myself if she'd have gotten hurt. Though as pale as she is, I might need to have her looked over when the ambulance gets here. She's really taking this to heart.

The doorbell rings again, and I hurry to let in more officers. My head spins with all the conversation. Whit returns to the tunnel with two uniforms, a man and a woman. The door to the yard opens, and three police officers come inside, deep in conversation.

I step in front of them. "What's going on?"

The tallest of the group turns to me. "Still trying to find their location from above." Then they hurry toward the front door.

Struggling to take a full breath, I stand next to my niece. "Do you want to go lie down? Or join Gretchen at the beach?"

She shakes her head no. "I'm not leaving."

"You should eat. You look—"

"No." Her brows draw together. "I'm staying here. I won't even go to the kitchen."

"Are you sure you're okay?"

Her eyes shine with tears. "I'm *fine*."

"Okay." I take a deep breath and consider my wording. "I'm here if you want to talk."

She doesn't respond.

I'm tempted to go into the tunnel, but I won't get far. Not with all the uniforms bustling around. There's no way they'll let me in given part of it has already collapsed. But I need to check on Graham, to see him with my own eyes.

Whit comes back inside. "Got any bottled water I can bring to them?"

"Yeah. Hold on." I race to the kitchen and fill my arms. "You guys can have as many as you need. We have more if you need them."

"Thanks." He takes the plastic bottles and turns to the tunnel.

"Hey, Whit?"

He glances back at me. "Yeah?"

"Tell the detective we're rooting for him."

Whit gives a slight nod before disappearing into the darkness.

Silence settles between my niece and me, other than the occasional sounds of police radios and conversation as they move around from the tunnel to the outside.

After a few minutes, Ember glances at me. "You called him Graham." Her tone makes it sound like a question. A really important one.

My stomach knots. She's picked up on the fact that there's something between Graham and me, and that I've been keeping it from her. I swallow and nod. "I wasn't sure if I should tell you, but we've seen each other a few times. Nothing serious. My focus is on you, not dating anyone. I don't even want a relationship right now."

She stares ahead, and I'm not sure she even heard me.

"Ember?"

"My birth dad's name is Graham."

Time halts. Everything spins around me. I lean against the wall for support. "You ... your ... I thought you didn't know anything about him."

She chews on her lower lip. "I didn't. But then I found a letter in my mom's room. She told me everything she knew about my dad. It wasn't much, but his first name is Graham."

So many questions swirl in my mind, but nothing coherent comes from my mouth.

Ember plays with her ear.

Her ear. The same habit I noticed from Graham.

She takes a deep breath. "I didn't say anything because I wasn't sure if I wanted to find him or not. I mean, he might not want anything to do with me. He doesn't even know I exist. The guy probably has a family and I would just mess it all up. Piss off his wife. Upset his kids."

"He might be happy to hear from you."

"That could be worse!" A single tear slides down her face.

I wrap my arms around her. "Why would that be?"

"Mom said he was going to school across the country. He might want to pull me away from my whole life here. From Gretchen." She sighs. "From you."

"I wish you'd have told me. I'd be more than happy to help you look into this."

"Do you think *he's* my dad? The detective?"

"I suppose anything's possible, but it's unlikely."

Or is it? I step back and study her, picturing Graham's face. Their hair is almost the same color. They have the same gold flecks in their irises. Their noses and chins are strikingly similar now that I think about it.

"Why don't you think it's likely?" She frowns.

"He's a lot younger than your mom, for starters." I do the mental math. "He'd have been eighteen when you were born. That's eight years younger than your mom, and I never once saw her date a younger guy. In fact, her penchant for older men drove Dad crazy. It was the one thing she did that didn't make them sing her praises."

Ember doesn't say anything.

"Are you okay?"

She takes a ragged breath. "My dad *is* eighteen years older than me. They had a quick fling, and Mom didn't learn much about him other than his first name and the fact that he was heading across the country to start college."

I choke on air. "Are you serious? Where is this note you found?"

"It's in my room now."

My knees wobble. I press my palm against the wall for support.

"Do you think it's him?" Ember's voice wavers. "He could've come back after he got his degree. Did the detective go to school on the east coast?"

"I don't know. What I do know is that he graduated high school fifteen years ago."

"You know that for sure? How?"

I look away. "I went to his class reunion with him."

"You what? And you didn't tell me?"

"I didn't realize it was so important. And it was all by chance. He called my company."

"Wait. You're not really dating him? He's just a client?"

"The lines are a little blurred."

"You're dating my dad?" Her eyes widen.

"We don't know that he's your dad!"

She holds up a finger. "His name is Graham." Then she holds up another. "He's the right age." Another. "He's from the area. He—"

"Okay, okay. We still don't *know*." I struggle to think of something to say that will help the situation. "Let's just focus on his safety for now. We can try to solve this mystery later—and I'm not talking about the moment he walks through the door. He'll need to recover first. Sounds like he needs stitches."

My niece scowls. "I'm not going to say anything right now."

"Okay, good. We need to talk about it after all of this."

Crash! Crash! Rumble!

My stomach drops to the floor.

"What was that?" Ember turns to me, face paling even more than before.

Screams sound from the tunnel.

An officer races out, gasping for air.

"What's going on?" I demand.

"The roof caved in! Several men are on the other side."

I step closer to my niece. "Is Detective Felton one of them?"

"Yes. We need you to exit the premises." He motions in the direction of the front door.

"What?"

"This is now a rescue mission. Go!"

His authoritative tone makes both Ember and me jump. Then I grab her arm and pull her away.

"Is he going to be okay?" she asks.

"Yes." As we pass the kitchen then the staircase, I look around for my mother. She's still nowhere to be seen.

"How do you know?" Ember demands.

"How do I know what?" I crane my neck to see if my mother is hiding on the other side of the steps or maybe upstairs.

She isn't.

My niece grabs my arm. "How do you know he'll be okay? You can't know that!"

I pull her outside into the sun's warm rays. "He's smart, he worries about safety."

"But the tunnel collapsed! He already needs stitches. What if—"

"Think positive."

"That's not going to help anything." She folds her arms across her chest.

"It won't hurt."

Chaos surrounds us as more police cruisers pull up, sirens wailing.

Neighbors are also crowded around, standing at the edge of

our property, staring and whispering. Dustin, the creepy history buff with perfect teeth, is in the middle of it all.

Then comes an ambulance. Everyone rushes around us, seeming to not even see us.

I collapse onto the lawn. Is Graham going to be okay? And is he really Ember's father?

29

Kenzi

E mber shakes next to me, and I pull her close, watching the excavator dig the earth. I'm still not sure how it managed to get so far into the woods. The driver obviously has some mad skills.

"Is he going to be okay?" Her wide eyes and fear make her look much younger.

My heart breaks for her. She just lost her mom and now she could possibly lose her dad.

No! She's not.

"Of course. He knows what he's doing."

"What about them?" She glances over at the construction crew tearing apart the ground.

"I'm sure they do, or the police wouldn't have hired them."

She frowns, pulls on her ear. "Do you think I'm crazy? Could he really be my dad?"

Now that I'm looking for them, all I can see is similarities between the two of them. My stomach knots at the thought of having feelings for the same person my sister was with at one time. No, they didn't have a relationship. But they did make a baby together. Maybe.

"Kenzi?"

"It's a possibility. Let's just focus on this for now."

She shivers. "I'm so cold."

"Let's stand in the sun."

Ember looks around. "Then we won't be able to see what they're doing."

"We can go to the house and get some warmer clothes. I'm chilly too."

She frowns. "I don't want to leave."

Neither do I, but it looks like I'm going to have to. "I'll run in. Is there a jacket or sweater in particular you want?"

"No. There's probably something on my bed you can grab. I also have a bunch in my closet."

"Your bed, okay. Anything else while I'm heading in?"

Ember wraps her arms around herself and shakes her head no, then steps to the side for a better look at the excavator.

"I'll be back in a few."

"Hurry."

"I will." I dash back to the house, greeting the officers and construction workers I pass. My hands and feet are cold—it's amazing the temperature difference between the woods and the sun. Once I step out of the trees, the heat wraps around me like a blanket, though it's going to take some time before the chill leaves me.

Once inside, I race to the tunnel entrance and stop before the steps, asking the cops milling around if there's any news.

Sergeant Whit turns to me. "We have people working from the tunnel and up on the ground, both trying to get to them."

"Are you still in contact with them?"

He nods. "From the sounds of it, they're pretty banged up."

"But they're going to be okay?"

"Felton might need some stitches or maybe a cast, but

neither of those guys is going down anytime soon. That much I'm sure of."

"Thanks." A little relief spreads through me as I spin around, eager to get a hoody on—maybe two. My hands are still cold.

Before I turn toward the staircase, I stop.

Chink, chink, chink.

I hesitate, listen. Hear another noise. It's too loud to be coming from the tunnel. And besides, it sounds like it's coming from Dad's office. It's probably just Mom, and that's enough for me to head for the stairs.

But then I turn around. I need to check out the sounds. Quickly, though. Ember needs her hoody and I want to be there when the crews rescue Graham and his partner.

Chink, chink, chink.

I definitely can't ignore that. It could just be my mom, or even someone working to get to the cave-in, though I don't know why they'd be near the office.

My heart picks up speed as I make my way over. It's enough to make me forget how cold I am.

Chink, chink, chink.

I've never heard the noise before today. My mind races as I step into the office and look around.

Nothing looks out of place. But that means nothing around here.

I walk around, checking out every small crevice.

Chink, chink, chink.

The noises are louder in here. But they aren't coming from the room. Where?

Holding my breath, I wait.

The second hand on Dad's clock moves in slow motion. I can't believe that thing is still going after so long. Could Mom have been replacing the batteries all this time?

Chink, chink, chink.

I straighten my back and focus. It's coming from the left side of the room. Nothing's over there aside from a bookshelf. There isn't a room on the other side of the office.

Is the noise somehow bouncing off the walls and ending up here from the tunnel?

Seems like a long shot.

I creep over to the bookshelf and cup my ear. Can't hear anything.

Chink, chink, chink.

It's louder here. But there isn't anything to cause the sounds.

Then I hear something that sends a shiver down my spine.

Muffled voices. From a bookshelf.

That's not possible. It's a shelf full of books. And there are no such things as ghosts. No. Such. Things. No, I can't explain the occasional giggles I hear, other than my mind conjuring up memories.

But there has to be an explanation. Like Mom sneaking in through a dangerous tunnel from the Prohibition. Not that it could explain *this*, but something like that.

Chink, chink, chink.

"Hello?" My voice barely comes out a whisper.

My pulse drums in my ears, making it so I can't hear anything else. I lean on the shelf for stability.

Something catches my attention. The spine of one book reads *Jack*.

My uncle? Brother? Or someone else, since it's clearly a well-loved family name.

I pull on the book. It sticks, but then the top pulls toward me.

Creak!

The entire shelf shakes. It moves toward me. Opens like a door.

My mouth falls open in shock.

The shelf continues moving toward me. I jump out of the way just before it hits me.

I stare, hardly able to believe my eyes.

A door disguised as a shelf. It's so cliché, but at the same time, so brilliant. Who would ever suspect it? I certainly never did.

The question is, what was my dad hiding?

Chink, chink, chink.

I'm about to find out.

My mind runs wild with ideas, but I have no clue. I pull out my phone, not sure if I'm going to need it to call for help or to get pictures of something nobody will ever believe.

I step into what looks like a hallway. Dust clings to the faded paint, and floorboards creak under my weight.

My breath hitches when voices sound again.

How is this possible? People are in here? It can't be. Must be a recording of some sort. Yeah, that's it. It has to be.

I hold still for a few moments and watch my phone shake in my hand. I'm going to be useless if whatever I find is dangerous.

I should've gone upstairs to get the hoodies.

Too late now. I'm in too deep.

Shadows move up ahead.

Shadows.

I'm an idiot. I should turn around now.

I keep going. The hall is short.

It leads to a room. Looks like a cross between the movie room upstairs and a boy's bedroom.

But that isn't what's crazy.

My mom is holding the hand of some guy at least half her age with shaggy hair and wild eyes. They're sitting on a bed with cowboy bedding. The guy is staring at me. Mom is fussing with his shirt.

"What's going on?"

My mom turns to me, her eyes wide. "Mackenzie."

I don't bother correcting her. "What are you doing?"

"This isn't what it looks like."

"I don't even know *what* I'm looking at!"

She rises and quickly looks back and forth between me and the man. He looks like a younger version of my dad.

"What are you two doing in here? And what is this place?"

The man stands, still staring at me. Doesn't say anything.

I narrow my eyes at my mother. "Explain yourself!"

"I ... your ... he ..." She clears her throat. "Let me start over. This is your brother, Jack."

"Jack's alive?"

He perks up, takes a step toward me.

Mom blocks him. "Jack, no."

He says something, but I can't tell what.

"Mom?" I fumble with my phone, ready to take pictures. "Why is my brother living here?"

"It's a long story."

"Then give me the short version! I need to get out there and check on Graham. Your tunnel collapsed on him!"

She lets go of Jack's hand. "What?"

"Long story. You first."

"They were going to take him away. Lock him up! We couldn't allow that. He's our son!"

I look around. "Isn't he locked up here?"

"Yes, but at least he's home. Safe with us. Not with those doctors, and not in a jail."

"Jail?" I look him over. He's at least as tall as my dad was, and he had been a hulk of a guy. If Jack's hair was cut and he wore nicer clothes, he could easily have been my dad's twin. There's no doubt about him being a Brannon. My brother.

"Why did they want to lock him up?" I back up a few steps.

My brother continues staring at me. Not that I could blame him—he likely hasn't seen another person in ages.

Mom motions for me to sit in a recliner across from them.

I don't budge. "I'm good here. Tell me what's going on. Ember's waiting for me, cold in the woods."

She grimaces. "Jack is a good boy. He just doesn't know his own strength, that's all."

"What does that mean?"

"He's not like you and me. There were some complications at the birth, and they didn't have the advances in technology they do now. He was without air for a little too long, and it affected his thinking. Mostly his impulse control. He's a good boy."

"He's a middle-aged man, not a boy."

Mom puts her arm around him. "He's my boy. Be careful what you say around him. He's sensitive."

I study my brother—it's such a strange thought. The brother that I only recently found out about is actually alive.

His eyes are curious as he continues to take me in. Seeing me must blow his mind.

"Hi, Jack." I take a step closer. "I'm your sister, Kenzi."

"Kenzi." He reaches a hand toward me.

Mom's eyes widen. "Be gentle, Jack."

I inch closer and finally shake his hand. "It's nice to meet you."

"Nice to meet you," he repeats slowly and squeezes my hand.

Mom's mouth gapes, her stance tenses.

I meet her gaze. "Why did they want to lock him away?"

"Let's discuss this out there." She nods toward the hall, toward Dad's office.

"Kenzi," Jack says.

I wrap his hands in both of mine and look into his eyes. "I'll be back. I promise."

"Promise."

"Yes." I nod vehemently. "I'm glad to have met you."

"Meet you."

A lump forms in my throat, then I follow Mom to Dad's office after she settles Jack in with a streamed movie. She closes the shelf-door and pushes the book back into place like it's the most normal thing ever. Only then does she turn to me.

"Why have you been keeping him in there? How long has this been going on? Was he there my entire life? Did Claire know about him?"

Mom holds up a hand. "Slow down. I can only answer one question at a time."

"Why is he in there?" Spittle flies from my mouth, I'm so furious.

"So he could be home with us. He wouldn't survive in an institution—there's no way they would take care of him like his parents would."

I narrow my eyes. "If you didn't want him to go, why would he?"

She takes a deep breath. "He doesn't understand things the way we do. Didn't grasp his growing strength as he got older."

"What does that mean?"

Mom closes her eyes for a moment and leans on Dad's desk. "He never meant to hurt anyone. He thought he was playing. Now he knows he has to be gentle."

I tilt my head, pulse racing. "What did he do?"

She looks away. "He killed a little neighbor girl."

I gasp. "He what?"

"They were playing hide and seek, like they had so many times before. He was older, but mentally they were pretty well matched."

I back up until I come to a wall. "You raised Claire and me in the same house as a *killer*?"

"He can't get out! You were never in danger, not from him."

"Who did he kill?"

"It was years before you were born, you never knew the family. They moved away after the incident."

"The *incident*?" I balk.

Mom hugs herself, looking toward the shelf. "Jack didn't mean to hurt Billa. He didn't even know what he did. For years, he kept asking for her to come and play with him."

My breath hitches. "Billa?"

She looks at me. "Just like your imaginary friend. You never did tell us how you found out about her. Do you remember?"

My secret brother killed my apparently not-so-imaginary friend? Years before I ever met and played with her?

"Kenzi?"

"I need some air." I run from the room.

30

Ember

The too-big hoodie hangs down to my knees, but I don't care. At least it's warm. I hope the construction worker who lent it to me doesn't get cold, but he's busy shoveling dirt and appears to be sweating.

I glance around for Kenzi again. She left over a half hour ago, and my mind is offering me only crazy explanations. Like Grandma going crazy and setting off on a bloody rampage. Or one of the ghosts deciding it wants to be a poltergeist.

But it's probably none of those things. Maybe a journalist showed up, and my aunt is giving an interview. Or the cops could've stopped her to ask questions about the tunnel—not that she would know much. We haven't even gone in there.

"Got them!" someone shouts.

My heart leaps into my throat. I pull the hoodie closer and hurry over to the site.

One of the policemen puts his hand out.

I sigh. If only I could tell him the detective might be my dad.

But I have to talk to Graham first. I still can't believe his first name is Graham. And that my aunt has been seeing him. I can't decide if that's cool or gross. Maybe both. I mean, in an ideal world, we could all be a family. Or things could get weird really fast. And even though he's a nice guy, that doesn't mean he wants to be a dad. Seriously, who dreams of being a single parent?

I truly hate all the unknowns. There are a million questions flying through my mind. Most of them have answers I don't want. Like, what if Graham thinks I only want money? Or what if he doesn't like me? Or if he denies ever having known my mom? He could do that—he was the detective on her murder investigation and never once said anything about having ever met her.

It could all be a coincidence. I know how many Grahams there are. I've done my research. But there aren't many in *this* part of the country. He's the first I've met.

Kenzi runs toward the woods, pulling me from my thoughts. She's not carrying any clothing. "You're never going to believe this!"

"They got to them, I know!" I point to where the cops and construction crew are working to pull out the two policemen, one of whom might be my dad.

She gives me a double-take. "They did?"

"That's not what you were going to tell me?"

Kenzi pulls her attention from the workers back to me. "Jack's alive!"

"My uncle? Or yours? And why does this matter when my *dad* could be over there?"

My aunt puts her hands on my shoulders. "My brother has been in the house this whole time!" She glances back in the direction of the house.

"Since we moved in?" I try to process what she's saying, but Kenzi's not making any sense.

"No! Before that. Since he was a kid. He's been locked in a secret room."

"That isn't possible." I shake my head. "The house was abandoned for *five* years. Nobody could survive that long locked up."

"Think about it." Kenzi squeezes my shoulders. "Your grandma has been sneaking in. Why else would she be so adamant about returning? Traveling through a dangerous tunnel? Sneaking out of the facility?"

I step back and lean against a tree for support. "This is all too much. In the matter of about an hour, I've discovered that the detective could be my dad and now this. What else do you want to throw at me? Grandpa's really alive too? Or maybe my mom?"

She frowns, pain in her eyes. "I'd do anything to bring them both back, but we both know that can't be done."

I close my eyes and take several deep breaths before looking at my aunt again. "You're saying a grown man has been living in our house since we moved in?"

"Yes, and just as we've been unaware of him, he's had no clue about us being there either."

A chill runs down my spine. "Where has he been staying? Where's the secret room? On the third floor? That would explain a lot of the sounds. Or has he been in his old bedroom? That would explain people seeing the light coming on at night."

"The room is attached to the office."

Her words take the breath from me. "Down in Grandpa's office?"

"Right. Doesn't explain anything. In fact, it makes it all creepier."

I arch a brow. "How?"

She looks away. "My childhood imaginary friend had the same name as" —she hesitates— "well, as a girl who died."

"What aren't you telling me?"

"Jack accidentally killed her."

I struggle to find words. "The giggling?"

Kenzi picks at a nail.

I start to say something.

But she stands up straight, looking past me. "He's out!"

"What?" I whip my head around fast enough to give myself whiplash.

Sure enough, three men are pulling out the detective. My dad. Maybe my dad. "I have to see him!"

She grabs my arm. "Don't say anything to him yet."

"I won't. It's clearly not the right time."

Kenzi breathes a sigh of relief. "We'll talk to him, get it all figured out. I promise. But we—"

"That's fine. I don't care. I just want to see him!" I race over, darting around an officer trying to keep me away from seeing my dad for the first time. Sure, I've seen him before, but never with the knowledge I now have.

He's been so close my entire life. If my mom had been a criminal lawyer, their paths might've crossed. She could've told us the truth herself.

As soon as I get close enough, I see three other men hoisting him up out of the hole. His pants are shredded and bloody. I cringe. My own legs ache at the sight.

He waves at me and smiles. "I'm fine." Then he pulls away from the others. Takes a step. Stumbles.

The other men grab him before he falls, and two medics race over with a stretcher. Everyone helps him on.

I dash over. "Are you sure you're okay?"

Kenzi catches up. "Graham!"

"I've never been better." He winces and reaches for his leg. "Actually, I *have* been better. But this isn't going to keep me down."

I frown. "You got hurt trying to keep us safe."

"All in a day's work."

"You mean vacation?" Kenzi lifts a brow.

"Technically, yes." The corners of his mouth twitch, and there's a gleam in his eye as his gaze meets hers.

She puts her hand on his and starts to say something, but the medics whisk him away as the other officers pull out my dad's partner. He's dirty but doesn't appear bloody.

Kenzi rests a hand on my shoulder.

I turn to her. "He could've died. Before I could've talked to him."

"But he didn't. I'll give him a call later and see when we can visit. Sound good?"

"I guess that's the best we can do for now."

"Yes. He needs to recover before we hit him with this."

I hate to admit she's right. It's not fair to him.

"Now, are you ready to meet your uncle? It's high time he sees the light of day."

I'm not sure I'm up for it, but I agree anyway. My uncle Jack has probably been through worse than both of us combined.

31

Kenzi

M y heart races as I lead Ember to the house. If I'd been thinking, I never would have left Mom with Jack. She's already hidden him away from the world for three or four decades, what's going to stop her from moving him? If she wants my brother all to herself, she could have already left with him.

Ember catches up with me. "Why are you running?"

"No time to explain!" I weave around officers and medics in the yard and turn the knob on the back door.

"He's been there for all this time, what's the hurry?" She gasps for breath.

"That's exactly the problem!" I race down the hall toward the library. It's the shortest route.

"Huh?"

"I'll explain later." I hope we're not too late. What if I've failed my brother? I actually have a living sibling, and I can't risk putting him in harm's way.

I offer up silent prayers as we near my dad's office.

The shelf that opens to the hidden room is closed.

My heart sinks. But it isn't necessarily bad news.

Jack could still be in there.

"Where's the hidden room?" Ember looks around.

"Here." I pull on the book titled *Jack*.

Creak!

Ember gasps as the shelf moves. "Whoa! It's like *Scooby Doo*."

I just nod and wait for it to stop. "This way."

We hurry down the little hallway and come to Jack's room.

He's still watching the movie Mom put on for him.

My mom is nowhere to be seen.

He turns to me. "Kenzi."

"It's so good to see you, Jack. Is Mom here?"

He shakes his head. "She left with you."

Relief floods me. I don't know what she's doing, but I'm not going to let Jack remain locked up another moment.

Jack gives Ember a quizzical glance then turns his attention back to the movie.

I clear my throat and nudge Ember closer. "Jack, I have someone I want you to meet."

He turns back to us, tilts his head. "Claire-bear?"

The air leaves my lungs. He knew our sister?

Ember shakes her head. "I'm Ember. Claire was my mom."

I wince at her speaking of Claire in the past tense, but it doesn't faze Jack.

"Ember." Jack smiles. "You're like my Claire-bear. All grown up."

"How old was Claire when you last saw her?" Ember asks.

He looks deep in thought and scratches his smooth chin.

Who has been keeping him shaved? Mom or him? But that's got to be one of the least important questions to ask.

Jack turns back to the movie.

"How old was Claire?" Ember asks again.

"Maybe he doesn't remember, or it might stress him out," I whisper.

Her eyes widen. "Oh. I didn't think of that."

My brother turns back to us. "Don't remember. She was my Claire-bear."

Tears sting my eyes, and Ember wipes hers.

I clear my throat. "Jack, do you want to leave this room?"

He turns to me, his brows furrowing. "I can go?"

"We'll take you out there."

Jack looks around. "Did Mom say it's okay?"

I grit my teeth. "She'll be happy for you to get some sunlight."

His mouth gapes. "I want to go outside!"

Ember leans closer to me. "Was he always like this, or is it from being locked up for so long?"

"From what your grandma said, he's always been like this."

"So sad. I can't believe she kept him in here like an animal!" Her brows draw together.

"You and me both." I put my hand on her arm. "Let's focus on getting him outside, then we can talk with her."

Ember's expression tightens. "I just can't believe it. Are all the Brannons horrible? The way our ancestors treated their servants, the science experiments, now *this*. Grandma's behind it! Grandpa had to have known. Didn't he?"

"I would assume so, but maybe she hid it from him too."

"This place is right off his office! The one I was almost never allowed in."

My body tenses. "I know. I rarely came in here either. Now we know the real reason."

Her face reddens. "I don't want to be a Brannon anymore!"

"Why don't we calm down and talk about this?"

"There isn't anything to discuss!"

I take a deep breath, glance at my brother who is back to watching the movie, and give Ember a hug. "This is all a shock,

I know. But keep in mind, we're not all monsters. Jack seems sweet, you're good, and so was your mom. We can make the Brannon name into something better. But let's focus on Jack. He's been in this room for at least thirty or forty years. We need to get him outside."

She wipes tears from her eyes and nods. "You're right, but if it turns out the detective is my dad, I'm changing my last name to Felton. I'm done with all of this!"

"Okay. But remember, we need to give Graham some time to recover before we bring this up."

"I know." She's quiet for a moment. "Actually, you know what? I can't deal with any more change in my life. I don't want to talk to him about this."

"You don't?"

"No." She crosses her arms.

I start to say something but then remember how stubborn I was as a teen. If I try to convince her otherwise, she'll just dig her heels in deeper. And besides, she'll probably change her mind five times before making an actual decision. "Okay. It's all up to you." I turn to Jack and raise my voice. "Did you say you're ready to go outside?"

"Outside!" He bolts to his feet and grins. "Are we really going?"

"We are. Do you need anything?"

He wrings his hands together and looks around. "Do I? Is it snowy?"

My heart aches. He doesn't even realize it's summer. I shake my head. "It's a beautiful summer day. But there are a lot of people in our yard and house right now. Is that okay with you?"

Jack pulls on his hair. "Like a party?"

Ember and I exchange a glance. She nods to him. "Yeah, but a party with police officers and medics."

His mouth forms an O shape. "Policemen? I love policemen! Can I meet one?"

At least he isn't fearful of people. I smile. "Sure. They're really nice. I bet we can find someone who will be really happy to meet you."

"Oh boy! Let's go." Jack hurries over and gently wraps his hand around my arm. "I want to meet the policeman."

I nod for Ember to walk on the other side of him, and we manage to get down the narrow hall single file, linked together.

When we step into Dad's office, Jack whips his head around. "Is Dad here?"

"No, sorry."

"He's been gone a long time."

"Yes, he has." I consider how to proceed. Mom may not have even told him Dad died. Probably hasn't, since Jack expects to see him.

Conversation sounds down the hall.

My brother tugs on my arm. "Policemen, Kenzi! Let's go."

Jack's so gentle, it's hard to believe he ever killed anyone—even accidentally. It makes me question my mom's story. Did she make up the whole thing about him killing Billa? Could she have been covering up the fact that she killed the girl? She knew that was my imaginary friend's name.

I don't have time to consider it further, as my brother is now dragging me down the hall, waving to the two cops standing at the entrance of the kitchen.

Whit turns down the hall from the direction of the tunnel. He arches a brow. "Who's this?"

My brother lets go of my arm, races over, and shakes his hand. "I'm Jack!"

I hurry over to them. "He's my brother."

Whit's brows draw together. "I wasn't aware you had a brother." He turns to Jack. "Did you just get here?"

"Yeah. I was in my room."

A medic comes over to me. "We're ready to leave, unless you have someone else we need to look over."

"Actually, could you check out my brother?" I introduce him to Jack, and the medic checks his vitals.

Whit gives me a confused glance. "Do you mind explaining? Felton gave me a solid briefing on your case, and I was under the impression your brother was a big fat question mark."

"He was. I actually just found out he's alive. Been living in a secret room off my dad's office this whole time."

"What? How long?"

I shrug. "Thirty or forty years."

"Let me see the secret room. Is it anything like that tunnel?"

"No, not at all. It looks fairly well-kept."

He nods. "I suppose that isn't surprising. He looks in decent shape. Why don't you show me?"

"Maybe Ember can show you. I don't want to leave Jack."

Whit holds my gaze. "Was he being held against his will?"

I frown and glance over at my brother. "I'm not sure he understood what his living situation was."

The sergeant pulls out a pad of paper and makes notes before nodding to Ember. "Show me the secret room."

Then the two of them head to my dad's office. I lean against the wall and watch the medic with Jack. He's chatting happily and seems to be enjoying himself. I look around for my mom, but she appears to be staying out of the way.

Probably doesn't want to get in trouble now that we know about her keeping Jack locked up.

The medic waves me over. "He's in great shape. Anything in particular you're concerned about?"

"No. I appreciate you taking the time."

"Glad to help."

Jack loops his hand around my arm again. "Can we go outside now?"

I glance over toward the office. Can't see Ember or Whit, so I send my niece a text to find us out front.

My brother *oohs* and *ahhs* at the front yard and takes a special interest in Mom's garden. I stay close and keep him engaged in conversation.

The sergeant comes out before too long and pulls me aside.

I motion for Ember to stay close to Jack.

"Where's your mom?" he asks.

"I don't know."

"Does she have a cell phone we can call?"

"No. She didn't have one in the retirement home, and I haven't gotten her a new one."

He leans a little closer. "Just to let you know, I'm going to have to take her in for questioning."

"Are you going to arrest her?"

"Can't say, but between this and her prints on the knife, we're going to need to hold her until we get some questions answered. What are you going to do with your brother?"

I tilt my head. "What do you mean?"

"He obviously has special needs."

"Right." I take a deep breath. "And he'll need a full medical and mental evaluation."

"Glad to hear you're already thinking about that. Is he going to stay here until you get that taken care of?"

"Yeah. I don't want to send him anywhere unless it's absolutely necessary. It would be a painful adjustment for him. And I think it's best for the three of us to be together, you know?"

Whit nods and hands me a card. "If you need anything, give me a call. I know Felton has been taking care of your case, so I'll take his place while he's out of commission."

"I really appreciate that."

I rejoin Jack and Ember. We spend a long time in the elaborate garden stretching from the front of the house to the backyard. It will take a lot of work to restore it to its former glory.

After a while, a commotion sounds near the front door.

Ember throws me a questioning glance.

I motion for her to stay with Jack, then I race to the front. Whit is escorting my mom to a police cruiser.

I should be crushed, but I'm overcome with relief. For now, I just want to enjoy watching my brother explore the property.

I'll worry about getting answers from my mother later.

32

Kenzi

My heart races as I look around the empty table. Conversation sounds in the background from other tables. Other people speaking with their jailed loved ones.

Not that I'm feeling much love for my mother at this point. I have to wonder if she ever felt anything for me at all. Between the lies and the criticisms, it seems unlikely.

But that isn't why I'm here.

All I want is answers. That's it. Then I'm walking away and hopefully never looking back.

A door opens, and my attention snaps in that direction. My mother walks out with a corrections guard. He nods my way, and she struts over, head held high.

Mom sits across from me, and neither of us mention her orange jumpsuit or the cuffs on her wrists.

I wait for her to say something.

She doesn't.

I have so many questions, I don't know where to begin.

"How is Jack?" she asks.

"Not locked up, that's for sure."

"That isn't what I asked."

"He's doing great, considering he's been unlawfully imprisoned for at least a quarter of a century. How long has it been, Mom?"

She sighs and looks away.

"He got a clean bill of health, both physically and mentally—no thanks to you. However, I do have to take him to counseling twice a week. But that isn't surprising, is it? The good news is he can live in the house with Ember and me. We've been helping him redecorate his new room. He picked one near mine. Oh, and he has lots of interesting stories." I lift a brow.

Mom's eyes widen, but she doesn't say anything.

"Did Claire know about him?"

Still no response.

I change the subject. "The police say there was no Billa."

She turns to me, her eyes wide.

"That's right. You lied to me about my brother killing a little girl. Why would you do that?"

"He did. That's why I had to lock him up—it was for his own protection. He wouldn't survive a day in jail. I'm sure of it now."

I hold her gaze. "The police have no records of a missing or dead child named Billa. You just said that to rattle me. Are you trying to send me back to the facility?"

Her brows draw together. "Better you than him."

My mouth falls open. But I pull myself together. "How did you keep him alive all those years?"

"He had his bedroom, a fridge, and a bathroom. Not to mention all the TV he wanted."

"You were in the memory care facility for *five years*."

She gives me a knowing look. "And I'd been sneaking out the whole time. You know that."

"How?" My voice rises. I can't help it.

"Brannon money will get you almost anything you want. I'm surprised you haven't figured that out yet. The owner was more than happy to look the other way for a price."

"Were you really scared of Richard? Or were you trying to avoid the slammer?"

Mom narrows her eyes.

"The police used the hair from a comb I found in Dad's office to prove the blood on that knife on the third floor belonged to Uncle Jack. You killed him, didn't you?"

"You don't know what it was like living with those men!" Her face reddens. "You barely got a glance of it living with your father. Multiply him by three and you won't even be close to what it was like living under the same roof as him, your grandfather, and your uncle—three men who thought the world owed them simply because they existed!"

"Why'd you do it? Why did you kill Uncle Jack?"

She sits up straight, her mouth forming a straight line. "You planning on testifying against me?"

"I want answers. I've been lied to my entire life. You owe me the truth."

Mom sighs, looks lost in thought for a moment. "He took advantage of me. Assaulted me. When I told him I was going to tell Bill, he threatened—"

"Wait!" My mind reels. "Billa. My dad went by Bill at home. Is that a coincidence? Tell me it is."

Mom's face contorts. "She's his daughter."

The words are like a slap to the face. "What?"

"Billa is your father's daughter—but not mine."

I rub my temples. "You said she *is* his daughter. Are you saying she's alive?"

"Unfortunately."

My mind spins. "I was actually playing with my *sister* all those times? Not an imaginary friend?"

"Half-sister," she mutters.

This can't be happening. "She lived in the house, and you let me think she wasn't even real?"

Mom glares at me. "Keep your voice down."

"Is that what happened?" I demand.

"She lived with us part time until her mother finally moved across the country. Then I told your father it was her or us. He couldn't have both anymore. He picked us."

I press my palms on the table. "Billa was a living girl, and you sent me to a mental hospital because I insisted she was real?"

Mom looks away.

It takes all of my self-control not to shake the woman. "The police knew about Jack, but why not Billa?"

"Your father was never listed on her birth certificate. I wouldn't allow it. But he still paid the mother until the brat turned eighteen, and he got visitation until I finally convinced that wretched woman to move."

"You're insane. You do realize that, don't you?"

"I wasn't before I met the Brannon men."

Everything in me wants to storm out, but I need one more question answered. "Where does the tunnel end?"

She turns back to me. "Out of all the questions you could ask, that's what you want to know?"

"It leads into my house, so yes."

"There are some caves in the woods, not far beyond our family cemetery. But after the collapse, I can't imagine the tunnel will do you much good."

I lean closer to her. "No, it won't. I had the hole filled in with dirt and replaced the grass over it. Also, the mirror has been sealed shut. Nobody will ever get in and out of the house that way again."

She shrugs. "It's just as well. Given the charges against me, I'm not likely to see the outside of these walls in my lifetime."

I straighten my shoulders. "Even if you do get out, you're

never stepping foot inside the house again. You won't see Jack either."

"You'd leave your mother to live on the streets?"

"You're resourceful. But like you said, it's a moot point."

Silence settles between us before she speaks. "I suppose this is the last I'll see of you too?"

"You can count on it."

"Do yourself a favor and get a real job."

"I *have* a real job."

She turns and calls for the guard.

"Wait. I have one more question."

"What?" Her forehead wrinkles.

"Whose son is Jack?"

She gives me an exasperated look. "Who do you think?"

My stomach knots. "Did Dad know?"

Mom shrugs. "He never said anything if he did."

"But you two named him Jack."

"He wanted to honor his dead brother."

The guard comes over and escorts my mom away.

I watch as she disappears behind the door, and I try to take in the news. It's going to take some time to process everything —if she told the truth.

I'm barely aware of traffic as I make the drive home.

Inside, the aromas of garlic bread and spaghetti sauce greet me.

My mouth waters, but I'm not ready to see anyone yet. I head upstairs to shower off the prison smell. By the time I'm in fresh clothes, I feel much better. I dab on some quick makeup, pull my hair back, then head toward the stairs.

Giggling sounds, followed by some muffled whispers. A door slams shut, despite the fact it's too cold for any windows to be open.

I don't know what the noises are, but at least I know I'm not crazy. Billa was actually real. I didn't imagine her, even though my parents let me think I did.

My priority is enjoying the meal my brother and niece are cooking. After that, I'll have to break the news about the third Brannon sister.

Disembodied whispers lead to deadly secrets... Read *The Darkest Garden* to discover more of the house's many secrets.

To be notified about the next book, join my new release notification list:

https://stacyclaflin.com/newsletter/

OTHER BOOKS BY STACY CLAFLIN

THRILLERS

Alex Mercer Thrillers

Girl in Trouble

Turn Back Time

Little Lies

Against All Odds

Don't Forget Me

Tainted Love

Take On Me

Danger Zone

Lady in Red

White Wedding

The Gone Saga

The Gone Trilogy: Gone, Held, Over

Dean's List

No Return

Brannon House

The Perfect Death

Family Secrets

Standalones

Lies Never Sleep

Dex

ROMANTIC SUSPENSE

When Tomorrow Starts Without Me

The Only Things You Can Take

When You Start to Miss Me

PARANORMAL ROMANCE

Dark Sea Academy

Mermaid's Song

Mermaid's Heart

Mermaid's Wish

Curse of the Moon

Lost Wolf

Chosen Wolf

Hunted Wolf

Broken Wolf

Cursed Wolf

Secret Jaguar

Valhalla's Curse

Renegade Valkyrie

Pursued Valkyrie

Silenced Valkyrie

Vengeful Valkyrie

Unleashed Valkyrie

The Transformed Series

Main Series

Deception

Betrayal

Forgotten

Ascension

Duplicity

Sacrifice

Destroyed

Transcend

Entangled

Dauntless

Obscured

Partition

Standalones

Fallen

Silent Bite

Hidden Intentions

Saved by a Vampire

Sweet Desire

Standalones

Haunted

Beauty

SWEET ROMANCE

The Hunters

Seaside Surprises

Seaside Heartbeats

Seaside Dances

Seaside Kisses

Seaside Christmas

Bayside Wishes

Bayside Evenings

Bayside Promises

Bayside Destinies

Bayside Opposites

Bayside Mistletoe

Bayside Dreams

Indigo Bay

Sweet Dreams

Sweet Reunion

Sweet Complications

Standalones

Fall into Romance

<u>**SHORT STORIES**</u>

Tiny Bites

AUTHOR'S NOTE

Thanks for reading *Family Secrets*. I enjoyed the first book so much, I worried couldn't possibly like this book as much. But I surprised myself by loving this one even more. It's always fun to get to know characters more and to explore their worlds — and who doesn't want to know more about the mysterious Brannon house? I'm excited to dig in deeper in future books and explore more of the many secrets.

A funny story about this novel is that I wrote *three* last chapters for this book. I ditched the first one, not liking the direction at all. Then I wrote a new last chapter, which ended up being the second-to-last chapter because it left too many loose ends. So I wrote the final last chapter!

If you enjoyed this book, please consider leaving a review wherever you purchased it. Not only will your review help me to better understand what you like—so I can give you more of it!—but it will also help other readers find my work. Reviews can be short—just share your honest thoughts. That's it.

Want to know when I have a new release? Sign up for new release updates:

http://stacyclaflin.com/newsletter/

I've spent many hours writing, re-writing, and editing this work. I even put together a team who helped with the editing process. As it is impossible to find every single error, if you find any, please contact me through my website and let me know. Then I can fix them for future editions.

Thank you for your support!

~Stacy

ABOUT THE AUTHOR

Stacy Claflin is a two-time *USA Today* bestselling author who writes about flawed characters that overcome unsurmountable odds. No matter how dark situations seem, there is always a sliver of hope—even if you have to search far and wide to find it. That message is weaved throughout all of her stories.

Decades after she wrote her first tales on construction paper and years after typing on an inherited green screen computer, Stacy realized her dream of becoming a full-time bestselling author.

When she's not busy writing or educating her kids from home, Stacy enjoys time in nature, reading, and watching a wide variety of shows in many genres. Her favorite pastime activity is spending time with her family.

For more information:
stacyclaflin.com/about